I0619526

RUINED: TOBIAS

Laurel Creek Series

USA Today Bestselling Author

HILDIE MCQUEEN

Ruined: Tobias

USA Today Bestselling Author
Hildie McQueen

Pink Door Publishing

Editor: Dark Dreams Editing

Copyright Hildie McQueen 2017
Print Edition
ISBN: 978-1-939356-85-7

ALSO BY HILDIE MCQUEEN

CHAPTER ONE

I F HE WAS going to die, Tobias Hamilton was going to be upright. The damn twinge in his chest had been present for the last few days and it was beginning to worry him. He slid from the bed and flexed in the mirror. He was in amazing shape. He lifted weights almost daily and then there was all the work around the ranch.

So, yeah, maybe his eating habits were not the best and he did like a cold beer or two at night. But, hell, didn't everyone? As if able to see his heart, he leaned into the mirror and stared at his chest. It looked normal.

"What are you doing?" Mimi, his fiancée, lifted to her elbow and looked at him with sleepy eyes.

"Got up cause my chests hurts." He waited for the hysteria. Three. Two. One.

"Oh my God!" Mimi shrieked. Her voice was so high-pitched his labs came running and began scratching and barking on the other side of his bedroom door.

After a long struggle to free herself from the sheets,

she hurried to him. "Let's get you to the hospital. At your age, you could be about to die of a massive heart attack."

"My age?" Tobias glared at her. "I'm not that damned old."

"Oh, I know…" Mimi said, turning in a circle. She kicked some clothes aside. "I need to find that bag with my new jeans. I'll go return them while you're at the hospital."

True she was ten years younger than him, he guessed about thirty-five or so, but that didn't make him "heart attack old".

"How old are you anyway?" he asked, shrugging on a t-shirt. "Can't believe we're engaged and I never asked."

She ignored the question and began dressing. "Is there even a hospital in Laurel Creek?" There was disdain in her voice. She hated his hometown and never pretended otherwise. "A reputable clinic maybe?" She shuffled to the bathroom. "I better get my makeup on. You should go call and make sure the clinic or hospital or whatever you have in this town is open."

If he were really dying, he'd be stiff as a board by the time she finished putting on makeup and doing her hair.

When he opened the bedroom door, the dogs jumped up and down, both seeming more worried about him than the woman in the bathroom.

He made sure to pet each of them. "I'm okay, boys. How about a snack?"

Both studied him for a moment as if gauging the

truth in his words. However, they couldn't ignore the fact he was about to feed them.

"Snack," he repeated. They hesitated until he took one step out of the bedroom and then raced to the kitchen, tails wagging.

When Mimi finally appeared, Tobias was on his second cup of coffee and prepared to head to town. The pang in his chest had gone and not returned. Probably just heartburn or something, he thought to himself. In town, he'd run a few errands that needed to get done before coming back to work.

"Ready?" she asked while sliding her purse strap onto her shoulder. "Did you call the clinic?"

He grunted as a reply and dangled the keys from his finger. "Let's go. I have errands to run. You should take the day and familiarize yourself with the local shops. There are a couple dress shops you might like."

She wrinkled her nose. "I thought you were having a heart attack. Don't you think you should get looked at?"

"Come on." He walked to the door with the dogs on his heels. Mimi gave them a wide berth. Tobias wondered if she and his pets would ever bond. Usually his tan labs, Scamp and Duke, loved everybody, but they seemed to sense Mimi wasn't fond of their kind, so they pretty much ignored her.

"I'll stop and see the doctor, just to be sure," he mumbled at the dogs that studied him intently.

Tori Romano stood with her mouth agape as tomatoes and onions rolled across the sidewalk and onto the street. This was the last thing she needed. The farmer's market was seriously lacking in vegetables that morning. It had taken forever to find the best of what they did have.

"You'd be passably pretty if you didn't scowl so much," Tobias, the bane of her existence, drawled. He stepped over a tomato and continued on past her.

"And people would think you're less of an idiot if you didn't open your mouth," she snapped, glaring at his wide back. Why she'd ever dated him and considered that man the love of her life was never clear.

"Looks like this one is still in pretty good shape," Eric Hamilton, Tobias' cousin, said, picking up a tomato and holding it up like a trophy. "That one over there is a lost cause," he continued pointing at one with the toe of his square-toed boot.

A few moments later, she'd recovered all but the one squished tomato.

"Your cousin could've helped." She looked down the street to where Tobias now stood, staring up at a building. "What is that dimwit doing?"

Eric cleared his throat. His gaze swept past her to his cousin and then back to her. "Um, well, he can't find her."

"Who?"

"You know." Eric shrugged, obviously uncomfortable. "His fiancée."

A chuckle escaped. It was a good cover up for the damned tightening in her chest every time she was reminded he was engaged. Not that it should matter much, but when he'd come to inform her of it, somehow, they'd ended up in bed. They'd not spoken of it again, pretending it never happened, which was fine with her.

He was not only an idiot but also her Kryptonite.

Tori placed her free hand on Eric's lower arm. "You don't have to tiptoe around me. Tobias and I are long over. It's been what, twenty years? I don't know why everyone acts as if our high school relationship just ended last week."

Eric frowned. "Probably because we all kept expecting you'd get married and have a happy ending, even after all these years."

It would never happen. If anything, they hated each other more and more as time passed. How he'd acted over her spilled vegetables was par for the course. If they'd had sex the night he'd come to inform her of his plans to ask someone to marry him, it was the result of him drinking, which he rarely did, and her having had half a bottle of wine.

Oh, and that damned television series of a super-hot Scottish man always taking his shirt off.

She sighed. "I better get inside. The sauce won't make itself." Tori gave Eric her best smile. "Don't forget law enforcement always gets a free meal at Victoria's once a week."

"I may just come for dinner today. Nothing like your lasagna to end the day on a good note." He walked away toward his cousin, still smiling.

The dim interior of her restaurant always made her feel at ease. Victoria's was named after her great-grandmother, who'd lived in Italy. Tori had also been named after the woman. The way her father described her great-grandmother, the woman was the reincarnation of Jesus' mother Mary.

Every time her father talked about his grandmother, her mother's eye rolls made Tori think the woman hadn't been all that saintly.

When her parents moved to Laurel Creek, Tori was a toddler. They'd opened the Italian restaurant because her father's cooking was in high demand. Once Tori was old enough, she'd worked at the restaurant on weekends and summers.

Over the years, Tori learned every secret and recipe from her father. They'd spent many a day listening to fifties music while stirring sauces and cutting pasta. Her father insisted she cook each item on the menu over and over until it came naturally.

So when he'd suddenly died of a heart attack, Tori was poised to take it over along with her mother. Now that her mother had passed, it was only her.

The year her father died had been the hardest of her life.

"Hey, Tori," Marco, her head chef and manager, greeted when she walked into the kitchen. "How's it going?"

She maneuvered around the kitchen to a metal table. "Dropped all these outside. My old market bag finally gave out." She dug the offending item from her back jeans pocket and held the tattered remnants up for him to inspect. "Too bad, I really liked this one."

"You get attached to shit too much," Marco said, walking over to inspect the food. "Things look okay."

"One tomato met a gruesome end."

"Rest its red soul," Mario said, grabbing a bowl and putting the items in it to rinse off. "I'm in the mood for pesto."

Tori lifted an eyebrow. "So pesto chicken over bow pasta will be the special?"

He nodded, already dismissing her. "You take care of the tomato sauce, while I work on my masterpiece."

It would be an hour before her pasta would be hanging out to dry, so she hurried to grab the canisters of flour and everything else she'd need.

They worked without speaking. Marco's favorite music played over the wireless system. She'd given up trying to talk him out of listening to what she termed "wedding-elevator music". Now, three years later, she sang along with Barry Manilow as she kneaded the dough.

"Delivery for Victoria Romano." A guy holding a vase filled with flowers entered. Her favorite flowers, daisies and yellow roses were framed with puffy baby's breath.

Tori's friend Allison, owned a quaint flower shop across the street, ever so often she'd send over flowers. Allison was such a good friend.

Had she sent the flowers after Tori had spilled all the details of her night escapade with Tobias? No doubt, her friend was trying to lift her spirits.

She was fine and didn't need to be cheered up. Sleeping with Tobias had been a huge mistake and Tori vowed to forget about it.

Still, it was a sweet gesture.

"You're new in town," she said to the young man who waited to hear where to put the flowers. "What's your name?"

"Jonathan Burnett, I'm from Billings. Just moved here to work with Mr. Hamilton."

"Come, I'll show you where to put them." She walked back into the front room holding her flour-covered hands up. "They will brighten up the entrance. I want them here at the hostess station."

He put them down. "I take it you know Mr. Hamilton?"

"Yep all of them. Most are cool, but it depends on which one you're talking about. There are tons of Hamiltons in this town."

He nodded. "Yeah, I learned that. Mr. Tobias Hamilton. He hired me to work out at the ranch."

"Yeah I know him," Tori replied, rolling her eyes and then stopped herself.

"Then why are you delivering flowers?"

He shrugged. "I don't start for a month. I came early to get a lay of the area. I do errands for a couple of shops. You need any help with deliveries or anything, let me know." He held out a piece of paper with his name and phone number on it. "Errands" was scribbled in ink on the bottom.

"I'll keep it in mind," Tori replied, not wanting to continue the conversation. If he asked why she'd rolled her eyes, she wasn't sure what her answer would be. She jutted a hip out. "Put it in my apron pocket."

BY NOON, EVERY seat in the restaurant was taken. Tori, along with Jessie, the only waitress, rushed back and forth to the kitchen retrieving plates and ensuring every beverage glass was refilled.

Across the room she spotted a foursome sliding into a booth by the window.

After a deep breath, Tori walked up to a table and smiled while placing glasses of water down in front of the four people seated in a booth. Her smile faltered just a bit when she looked around the booth.

Obviously, Tobias had located his fiancée, because the blonde was smashed to his side. He didn't meet her gaze but instead looked down at the glass of water. Across from him were Eric and Mindy, who owed the local coffee shop, Cuppa Joe.

"Your food is so good," Mimi, Tobias' new fiancée, exclaimed. "You should consider opening a second restaurant in Billings or Helena. Your talents are wasted in tiny little Laurel Creek." She gave her a wide-eyed doe look.

Tori tried to smile, but her face hurt. Instead, she reached for a pitcher and topped off the already full glasses. "I like it here fine," she replied.

"I'm sure she means it as a compliment," Mindy spoke up a bit too quickly. "Right Mimi?"

"Of course," the blonde said, her gaze moving from Tori to Tobias. "If it wasn't for my babe's ranch, we'd be gone already."

"One can only dream," Tori said and turned away. She caught Jessie's eyes. "Can you cover table nine for me?"

Jessie looked to Tobias' table and her eyes widened just enough to tell that she understood loud and clear. "Not a problem."

"I'll take four," Tori said, dashing past to take the table's order.

She kept busy ignoring table nine for the next hour, while the foursome lingered over lunch.

Tori went to the cash register to check out one of her tables. Just as she reached the counter, so did Tobias. His eyes were flat when looking at her. "Left money on the table for your tip."

Eric and the two women had already walked out, making her wonder why he'd lingered. "Okay," she replied and counted out change for the other customers. The entire time, Tobias remained there. Once the customers from her table walked out, she met his gaze again.

"What?"

"You accepted my apology then?" He looked to the flowers.

If it weren't for other customers being there, she would have yelled. Instead, she spoke through clenched teeth. "What are you talking about?"

He picked the note from the flowers and put in in her apron pocket. "Read it." With that, he strolled out.

"You look flushed. It's a good thing the lunch crowd is almost done." Jessie rounded her and pecked at the register keys. "Are you feeling okay?"

Tori refused to think of the fact that Tobias had sent her flowers and apologized for something. Hell, if he took to apologizing for each time he'd done something wrong, Allison would be a millionaire. Whatever was this about?

A part of her wanted to crumble the paper and throw it out without looking at it. The last thing she needed was to have him on her mind. The man was like a mite. He had a way of getting under her skin, like a bad rash.

Tori was scratching her arm when Allison waved through the window. The pretty wild-haired woman scowled and Tori motioned for her to come inside.

"Oh my goodness. I can't take it. I was hoping not to have to walk inside." Allison pretended to swoon. "It smells like heaven in here."

"You always say the same thing. Want to eat a late

lunch with me?"

"And you always feed me, which means I am going to be your best friend forever."

Tori went to the drink station and poured two glasses of water and then looked through the kitchen door. "Two small salads, one lasagna and one pesto special," she called out. Then she turned around and went to an empty booth and put the glasses down.

Although they'd already paid, her last table remained and she made sure their glasses of water were refilled. Tori ensured they didn't need anything and listened as the older couple described their drive across Montana. They owned an RV and were having the time of their lives. Their bright smiles made Tori's heart happy. "I hope you decide to stop back through and tell me about the rest of your adventure."

The couple quickly agreed, promising to bring pictures.

Soon, there was only one table with a couple of women who had notebooks out and had finished their meal. They were either studying or doing some sort of business and had asked Jessie for coffee and to be left to themselves for an hour.

"They tipped me twenty dollars just to remind them to leave in an hour," Jessie said, holding up the bill with a smile. "Cool, huh?"

Tori agreed. "Very cool."

She slid across from Allison. "So why did Tobias send me flowers. And more importantly, why didn't you tell him to shove them up his…"

"Because like anyone else, he is a customer and I do what I'm paid to do. Besides, they are so pretty." Allison admired her handiwork. "I love yellow, don't you?"

"They are very pretty. But really, Allison, what the hell did he say? I am not in the mood to deal with him. To make matters worse, he and his dingbat fiancée just left. They had the nerve to come here for lunch. Here!"

Tori got up at hearing Marcos' call.

"I have some juicy gossip. You're going to die laughing. That Tobias is a riot," Allison said as Tori walked away.

How did this turn into a Tobias chat? Tori had no desire to hear about his latest dumb action. It was time to move one. What she needed was a day to herself. There had to be a single, attractive man she could date and give the town no reason to think she was available and waiting for Tobias. Because she absolutely was not waiting on that idiot.

The sooner Laurel Creek accepted the fact she was dating someone and he was about to be the Mr. to Mrs. Bimbo, the better things would be.

Mind made up, she sat back down as Allison looked up. "Do you want to go to Billings with me this weekend?"

"Sure, but let me tell you what happened at Shooters this weekend. Tobias…"

"I don't want to know what he did. He's an idiot and he's engaged and I don't care."

Allison waved her words away. "He told Mimi that she was his going to be his next ex-wife. She started screaming and stormed out. Left him there."

Allison continued the tale. "Taylor took him home after he showed up at our door half-dressed and a bit too tipsy to drive himself home. He kept talking nonsense about how you and him were going to end up together one day."

"That was the night he...we..."

Allison's eyes widened. "Oh, well shoot. I didn't think about that. So you undressed him then?" Her friend giggled.

"It's not funny. Besides, I told you, I had drunk half a bottle of wine and he was...tipsy."

"Mmm, hmmm," Allison lifted lasagna to her mouth. "I'm going to pay for this lunch. It's too good to be free."

Tori picked at her plate and then ate a forkful.

The chicken pesto was amazing. She made a mental note to ask Marco to make it a regular item for Tuesdays. She glanced across to the women, who were still engrossed in conversation. "That's why you have to help me find a boyfriend. I need to stop leaving any possibility of Tobias waltzing through my front door."

"I thought you hated him," Allison said. She continued before Tori could reply. "Then again, it's a thin line between love and hate."

"There is no love in it."

"Then why did you sleep with him and why did he

say you and him are going to end up together. Honestly, Tori, if you just tell him how you really feel, he won't make the huge mistake of marrying Mimi."

Tori let out a long breath and ate more of the delicious food.

"I couldn't care less about Tobias Hamilton. We slept together because hate sometimes causes chemistry. But like most chemical combinations, we would probably explode if we ended up together."

Allison motioned to her with the fork she held. "Did you read the note?"

Reluctantly, Tori dragged the crumpled piece of paper from her apron pocket. She scowled at the familiar slanted handwriting.

"Sorry for coming over drunk. Sex was great."
Tobias.

Tori let out a breath and shook her head. "The sooner he gets married and leaves town, the better."

CHAPTER TWO

"HEY, THERE." LEAH plopped down across from Tori at Cuppa Joe, the coffee shop down the street from her restaurant. "I hear you got flowers."

Sometimes Tori wondered what it would be like to live in a bigger town where everyone didn't know her business.

"Yep. If it wasn't for the fact they are pretty, I would behead them and send the stems back to the dumbass."

The coffee shop owner, Mindy, neared and refilled Tori's coffee cup. "I love yellow flowers. I haven't gotten flowers in a long time." She sighed and went to the next table.

"You do realize nothing will ever happen between Tobias Hamilton and me, don't you?" Tori tapped her fingernail on the tabletop for emphasis. "He's engaged to be married and if I'm lucky, that squeaky-voice Mimi will convince him to move to Billings."

Leah narrowed her eyes, and tossed her always-perfect hair. "I hate to think of it. So I prefer to remain in denial. You two are meant to be. Everyone knows it except for you…and Tobias."

"Explain to me why? We don't get along. I broke his heart when I ended things just as he went to a war zone. Everyone should hate me for that."

"It's been many years. We've forgiven you."

"Oh. My. God." Tori stood up and picked up her toasted bagel. She really hated leaving the coffee, but if anyone else brought up the damned flowers, she was going to scream.

"Hey, Sugar. You don't have to leave because of me." Of course, the timing as usual was horrible. Tori swung to face Tobias.

"Why the hell are you always in town? Don't you have a ranch to run? Your cows must be starving and your dumb horses are probably standing knee deep in shit."

When he opened his mouth to talk, she stuffed the half-eaten bagel into his mouth. With a huff, Tori rounded him and left the coffee shop.

It was too early to go to the restaurant. Since it was Monday, they only opened for dinner. She could always work on accounts or organize the pantry. However, she'd promised herself a day off. The plan was to spend time at the coffee shop and catch up on social media, and then she planned to go to the shelter and see about adopting a small dog. Since her own dog had died, she missed having the companionship of a pet to keep company with in the evenings.

"Shit," she grunted, realizing she'd left her laptop on the table in the coffee shop. She turned to see Leah and Tobias standing on the sidewalk talking. He held the laptop under his arm and a coffee cup in the other hand.

She neared, making sure to keep her eyes averted. It was best not to look Hamiltons straight in the eyes. They had some strange kind of pull that made stomachs flip and hearts race.

"What?" He turned.

"My laptop," Tori replied, looking at Leah, who seemed to be fighting the urge to laugh.

Tobias blew out a breath. "Good thing you're back. Thanks for the bagel. I need to talk to you."

Her heart stopped and she couldn't breathe. It was time to get away from him pronto. "About what?"

"Come back inside. Finish your coffee."

Leah turned to look across the street. "I'm going to see if Allison has a blouse I can borrow." She practically sprinted away. The Traitor.

Since he still had her laptop hostage, Tori had not choice but to follow him back inside.

TOBIAS WASN'T SURE exactly why he'd not just called instead of speaking to her in person. The subject was probably going to set her off. Hopefully, the fact they were in public would help. Hell, who was he kidding? They always fought in public.

In actuality, he needed to keep away from her. Just

looking into her deep brown eyes made him want to drag her to the closest bed, get lost in her and not come up for air until they were both sated. She was the one who'd broken his heart and thanks to Tori Romano, he'd never trust a woman as long as he lived.

"I ah…I need the ring back." He spoke as soon as she sat down. Her eyes widened and then narrowed.

"What ring?"

He leaned forward so that he could speak in a low tone. "You know what fucking ring. Don't give me crap about it, Tori. Just give it back."

Her lips pressed into a tight light and the little pert nose flattened when her nostrils flared. "I have no flippin' idea what the hell you're talking about. Give me my damned computer and get out of my face Hamilton."

The patrons at a nearby table, an older pair of ladies, looked to them without blinking. The eager expressions almost made him give Tori the computer and leave. "The engagement ring. I need it back."

Realization dawned and she blinked before opening her mouth to form a perfect "O". "Oh shit, I forgot about that. I tried to give it back to your mom."

"I know."

"She said to keep it."

A trickle of dread flowed down his spine. "What did you do with it?"

The ring had been in the family since his great-great-grandmother Lucille Hamilton. If Tori had sold it, pawned it or destroyed it, he wasn't sure what he'd do. If she said it was gone, he'd have to high-tail it out of the coffee shop, otherwise he would strangle her. Prison didn't sound so bad, however, when considering having to deal with his father's reaction if he found out.

Tori bit her bottom lip. "I'll look for it and send it to your mom."

"No," he gritted the word out. "You'll get it now and give it to me."

She huffed. "Give me my laptop."

"Not until you give me the ring."

"What do you want it for?"

Once again, he had to lower his voice so not to cuss in front of the eager beavers who continued to watch with fascination. "You know what I want the damned thing for. Stop screwing with me."

"I'm not sure I want to do anything for your rude ass." She yanked the computer from under his hand and marched out the door.

"What the hell!" Tobias yelled and got to his feet.

"Hey, Cuz," Eric Hamilton, the local cop and Mindy's new love interest, slid to block him from following Tori. "Calm down. Best not to go after her. Let me talk to her."

Frustrated to the point of the inability to form words, Tobias raked his fingers through his hair. "That woman will give me an ulcer. She is so damned annoying."

"Yeah, I can see that." Eric's gaze moved from his face to Tori who'd crossed the street and half-jogged to her house. "I'll have to ask her to join my team for the Laurel Creek Memorial Day fun run."

Tobias snapped his fingers in Eric's face. "Go talk to her and get her to give you the damned engagement ring before Dad finds out it's lost and has a coronary."

"I will, but I've got a cup of coffee and a muffin with my name on them." Eric walked around him and went to the counter. Mindy smiled sweetly at his cousin, her cheeks coloring. Those two were annoying too, Tobias decided and stalked out.

Mimi was leaning on her silver Mustang. She waved at him, her eyes darting in the direction Tori had gone. "Hey, there. I was about to walk into the café, but heard a commotion and decided to wait out here for you."

"Yeah, sorry about that. She makes me lose my temper."

"About that." Mimi gave him a pointed look. "I'm getting a bit tired that every time I turn around you and Victoria are in each other's faces."

Tobias decided it was best not to say anything. He was in a sour mood and it wasn't Mimi's fault. Instead, he nodded.

"I mean it. This is not how I want to spend our married life together. We have to talk."

The silent path wasn't going to work. So he took her arm and directed her to Allison's flower shop. They were supposed to pick flowers or arrangements or something. He'd come early in hopes of catching Tori and getting the ring back.

"Mimi, I promise to do my best to give her a wide berth. Avoid her at all costs from now on."

His fiancée wasn't about to be deterred from the conversation, and pulled her arm from his grasp. "It's impossible. This town is way too small for the both of you. We have to move to Billings. The sooner, the better. I think it's for the best. Think of our marriage, our future together, sweetness." She pressed her generous breasts against him and lifted to her toes to kiss him, her arms snaking around his neck. "Think about it," she insisted between kisses.

He didn't want to think. If Mimi knew him, she'd understand he was an overthinker and then ended up making the worst decision. So instead, he decided to make a spur of the moment decision. "Fine, yeah, it may be best for us to move away. My parents will be glad to have us closer. I'll start working on it."

"Yay," she exclaimed. "You can let Luke oversee the ranch, hire people to take care of the cows." Obviously, she didn't understand or care how much of a burden it would be on Luke.

Wrapping her arms around his waist, she urged him to walk to the flower shop. They made an awkward entrance through the door as Mimi didn't release his waist and they had to thread through the door one first and then the other.

Allison narrowed her eyes just for an instant. She smiled, but it didn't reach her eyes. Of course, she was firmly settled into the Anti-Mimi camp, but he didn't give a damn. Mimi was beautiful, sensual and he would never fall in love with her. It was enough that she aroused him and was great in bed. That was all he needed.

Love was for idiots.

THAT EVENING, TOBIAS hoped to relax and not do a damned thing. Other than a couple chores at the ranch, it would be a relaxing evening.

"I want to go to Bora Bora," Mimi informed him as she flipped through a travel magazine. They were in the kitchen of his ranch home. He studied his beer can, too bored with the conversation to reply. For the last thirty minutes, she'd said she wanted to go to at least fifteen places.

"I better get out and check on the horses. Wanna come?" he asked, knowing she'd say no.

She gave him a bright smile over the lowered magazine. Her blonde curls bounced as she shook her head with enthusiasm. Mimi did not like the outdoors unless it included a pool, beach, or some sort of fancy picnic.

"How about I stay here and wait for you. We can take a shower together and, afterwards, we can have some champagne out back. I love looking at the stars."

Admittedly, it sounded nice to spend time just relaxing with his future wife.

Why did he not jump at the idea? Instead, he wanted to go out to the stables and take his time with his horses.

The weather was nice and the animals spent more time outdoors than inside, but they still had to be checked on.

"Where did the dogs go?" Tobias looked around, realizing he'd not seen the pups in a while.

"They went outside an hour ago," Mimi pointed to the patio door. "Probably out running or something."

He stood and stretched. "I'll be ready for that shower when I get back."

CHAPTER THREE

"**W**HAT THE HELL? We were supposed to leave an hour ago. What happened to you? You look like shit!" His identical brother Luke stalked through the living room toward the kitchen. Tobias didn't bother answering. He'd forgotten all about their planned trip to Billings to a cattle auction.

He turned the volume down on the television and sat up. "I have a lot of shit on my mind. Spent all night with a cow."

"Mimi will be pissed if she finds out you called her a cow." Luke's tone was flat, but Tobias knew he was kidding.

The aroma of coffee followed the gurgling sound of the coffeemaker. He stood and went to the kitchen. "I'll be ready to go in a bit. Let me just wash my face."

"Nah, it's getting late, we can go next week." Luke watched the coffeemaker as if it would make the process go faster. "What happened?"

Tobias leaned on the counter and shrugged. "Hard

birth. Poor thing was stuck badly. Didn't think I needed to call a vet and, by the time I realized how bad it was, it was too late."

"Lost both?"

"Just the calf."

"Shit."

"Yeah."

Luke poured two cups of coffee. "I suppose it'll be a good day to hang out and help you with stuff around here."

Although his brother was a man of few words, he always seemed to know when Tobias needed a sounding board. And while there were times when Luke wouldn't say a word, just being able to share things was usually more than enough.

Tobias cleared his throat. "Do you plan to stay here for the rest of your life? Let this be it? Ranching, spending every day and night with horses and cattle?"

Instead of replying right away, Luke took a long sip of his coffee and looked straight out the sliding doors. It was obvious he was considering what to say. Finally, he met Tobias' gaze.

"There's nothing out there that's any better. This is where I belong." Luke studied him. "What's got you thinking different? You've always wanted to make this ranch successful and raise a family here."

He wasn't about to tell Luke about Mimi's request. It would seal her fate as the most disliked member of the family. "Lately, I've been feeling sort of stifled. You know, like I can't breathe fully and then there's so much of my past here."

"You mean Tori?"

Why the hell did he have to bring her up?

"No, not just Tori. I mean everyone trying to dictate my life. I know you all don't like Mimi, but she's the woman I'm going to marry. I don't need to see disapproval and judgment everywhere I turn."

A tennis ball rolling past his feet followed the sound of a dog's nails on the wooden floor. One of the dogs, Duke, sat in front of him and looked up. Tobias couldn't help but chuckle. "I'll let you out, but I'm not playing fetch right now."

"Why not?" Luke said, bending to pick up the ball and going to the sliding doors. "The dogs stifling you, too?"

"What the fuck?" He clenched his jaw, not sure what Luke meant by the comment and followed his brother and excited dogs out to the back deck. Luke bent to pick up a second ball and threw both.

The dogs barked and raced off. His brother turned with a scowl that probably matched his own.

"If you're not happy, it has nothing to do with Laurel Creek, the ranch or the people here. You need to ask yourself what's really going on."

Tobias let out a long breath. "Luke, I don't have to figure it out. It has everything to do with this damned place. Sometimes Laurel Creek is too small. Everybody knows your business."

The dogs returned, dropped the balls and, once again, stared up at them with expectancy. Tobias threw the balls this time.

"Sell the ranch and leave. See how happy that makes you. I'm letting you know now, I am not going to take it on. Make sure you give family the option to buy first. Oh, and fuck you." Luke walked off toward the stables.

What the hell was happening? How did he become the bad guy all of a sudden?

"Hello?"

One of his cousins walked out from the kitchen. It was Taylor. In a khaki sheriff's uniform, Taylor was in his element. Having gone through some formidable crap, it was strange how his cousin remained so steady, easygoing and, for the most part, normal.

"Came to see my dog."

Both labs ran up to Taylor and began jumping up and down. The man had a way with dogs, actually with most animals. Since he'd planned on marrying Allison, Taylor had moved into her apartment above the flower shop. Taylor and Tobias had decided it was best that the dogs remain together there at the ranch. Another thing he'd have to deal with if he decided to move to Billings was what to do with the dogs.

"How's home life?" Tobias asked. "I know you guys aren't actually married yet, but do you have any plans on where you two are going to live permanently?"

"Nah," Taylor replied while petting the dogs. "I kinda like staying in Allison's apartment. We're in the middle of town, so I can get to work in a hurry. It's relaxing."

Of course, his cousin could possibly be persuaded to move out to the ranch. The only deterrent would be all the work with the livestock. And then there was the thirty-minute drive into town.

"Yeah, sounds convenient. Wonder what it's like to not have to dedicate every living moment to animals."

Taylor studied him. "Burning out, Cousin?"

"A bit maybe."

Whenever Taylor had something on his mind, he walked in a circle, or sometimes paced from one end of a room to the other. He must have had a lot on his mind that morning because he was making some sort of zigzag pattern on the deck. Much to the dogs' delight and to Tobias' annoyance.

"Spit it out."

"She's not the right woman for you, Tobias. You need to think this through…"

"Enough!" Tobias got to his feet and made a slashing motion with his hands. "Leave me be. I need a day away from everyone and everything. I'm a fucking grown ass man. I can make up my own mind about who I marry. Damn it!" It was childish, but he stomped his foot.

When Taylor went to open his mouth, Tobias put both hands up. "Whatever you have to say can wait. I don't need it today."

He stormed from the deck and headed to the stables.

His horse was saddled and ready in record time.

Tobias mounted and allowed the animal the freedom to gallop wherever and as fast as it wanted.

A few moments later, he spotted Luke. The man had a way with horses, rode as if he were part of the animal. Luke, he was born to be in the saddle.

The sun was not quite straight up, but it made for a bright, sunny day. Tobias wasn't surprised when Luke rode to a group of wayward cows and began working with his ranch hands to herd the animals to a different pasture.

"Go!" He urged his own mount toward the others, not surprised when, moments later, the roar of Taylor's four-wheeler sounded and his cousin appeared on the horizon.

They worked for three hours straight and it was the best time Tobias had experienced in a long time. He, his brother and cousin had all been too busy doing their own things. He'd forgotten how well they worked together.

It could be that instead of being burned out, he missed the way things used to be. Instead of living with Taylor and Luke, he was alone. Instead of working with two men he trusted and loved, he had men who worked for him.

Sure it was a natural progression but, damn, it wasn't what he wanted. Family was important and it had taken so long to get Luke back in Montana. And now that he was home, he'd barely been there a few months before falling for Leah and moving to her ranch next door.

Taylor came up alongside. "I'm gonna go on ahead. I better get back to town." He grinned up at Tobias. "This was great." He saluted and took off, the four-wheeler at full speed.

"That idiot is going to roll that thing if he keeps that up." Tobias hadn't noticed his brother until Luke was beside him.

Tobias nodded. "Yeah, but he's pretty good handling the four-wheeler. Loves riding it." It seemed to be true, although it was hard to know if Taylor would have preferred a horse.

Taylor had been shot multiple times while working as a detective, in the city, and his body couldn't withstand horseback riding.

"I needed this," Luke admitted. "Great way to get rid of stress." He eyed Tobias. "Keeps me from wanting to punch your face in."

"Bring it," Tobias challenged. "You may be more muscular, but I'm quicker."

They were identical twins, but Luke had bulked up while he was gone. Tobias worked out, but was not as stringent with his schedule as Luke was.

"You'll work things out, Brother." In typical Luke fashion, his words hit home.

Would he?

"What the doctor say?" Luke asked, once again proving how small Laurel Creek was.

"That I need to change my eating habits and that I worked my chest muscles to hard." Tobias replied.

"Guess I'm not going to die yet."

They continued in silence until arriving at the stables. Once the horses were brushed down and loosed into the corral, they walked toward the house.

Luke went to his truck and looked at his phone. "I'm going to pick up a few things for dinner. Leah wants you to come over."

"Yeah. Okay." Leah seemed to be the only one who accepted Mimi, so he welcomed the time over at Luke and Leah's house.

FROM INSIDE THE coffee shop Mindy's heart skipped a beat whenever Eric came into view through the front windows. He walked across the street heading to the shop. So much had gone wrong in the last year that to have a bright spot was something she relished. It was hard to keep negative thoughts at bay and accept that, for once, something wonderful was happening.

The bell over the door jingled and she looked up with a bright smile, only to allow it to dim when noting it wasn't Eric, but an older couple who lived outside of town. "Hello Mr. and Mrs. Barnes. Haven't seen you in a while."

The woman neared the counter. "I have a doctor's appointment and convinced Gordon to come early so I could come here and then stop over at the flower shop."

"What a good idea. It's always fun to walk around

this street. Did you see the new gift shop that just opened?"

Something about Mr. Barnes' expression made Mindy stop talking and take a closer look at Mrs. Barnes. She was especially pale.

"Are you feeling all right?"

The woman's warm smile was endearing. "As well as can be expected. Today, I find out how many rounds of chemo I have to go through. Gordon is worried, but I'm not. I have faith it will all work out just fine."

"Of course it will," Mindy said with a firm nod. "Coffee and muffins are on me. Let's start off the day with a gift."

The couple placed their orders and sat by the window. Moments later, they were laughing about something and Mindy couldn't help but smile. Teresa and Gordon Barnes had been together as long as she could remember. Mrs. Barnes had taught elementary school and he'd been everyone's dentist. They were the best example of a wonderful marriage.

She let out a sigh.

"Good morning." Eric's deep voice cut through her like a hot knife into butter and her knees weakened. She glanced up at him.

Tall, broad-shouldered and in uniform, he was definitely eye candy. His hazel gaze moved over her, but he didn't meet hers.

"I didn't realize you'd arrived. How are things in town this morning? Is Laurel Creek safe and protected?"

She was babbling.

There was a slight lift to the corners of his mouth. He nodded and reached for the refilled travel mug that her helper handed to him. "Yep, all is safe and well." He didn't seem particularly happy to see her, nor did he act his usual flirty way.

Mindy touched his sleeve. "Is everything all right with you?"

"Couldn't be better." Eric met her gaze for a beat, then turned and walked out. That was also not like him. He usually found excuses to linger. Something was definitely wrong.

They'd been on three dates so far. Hadn't slept together yet, but the last date things had gotten especially steamy. Could it be that he was upset that she'd put a stop to things? She blew out a breath. Actually, it had been him who'd pulled away. He'd gotten a radio call or something. So their lack of intimacy wasn't it. Whatever it was, she'd have to find out.

Allison strolled in with a vase of flowers in hand. There was an "Enchanted Garden" card sticking out the top. "Hey, there. Got something for you." She grinned at Mindy. "It's from me. Advertisement."

Of course. She'd held her breath for a moment thinking they were from Eric. "I was hoping you'd realize your true feelings for me. No need to make excuses."

Allison giggled. "You see right through me." She looked around. "Where should I put them for the most visibility?"

"What about the table there?" Mindy motioned a table just inside the door. It was decorated and staged to look like a meal. It had a cup and plate on which there was a folded napkin across it. There was a small chalkboard with the special coffee flavor of the day. Allison rearranged everything, adding the small vase, and automatically it looked especially beautiful.

"You have such a touch with things," Mindy told her. "I have something to ask." She tugged her friend just outside the front door.

Mindy looked up and down the street to ensure that she would not be overheard. If one was going to be neurotic, it was best not to have witnesses. "Has Taylor said anything about Eric? He's acting strange."

Allison's eyes widened. "Strange like what? I thought you said your last date was fantastic."

"He barely said a word to me just a bit ago when he came in for coffee. Then he left. He never just leaves. He normally lingers for a bit and kisses me."

Allison frowned. "No idea what that's about. But I promise to interrogate my man and report back."

Biting her bottom lip, Mindy couldn't help but worry. "Find out what you can, please, but don't make a big deal about it. It may just be me being paranoid."

"You're the sanest person I know. If you sense something wrong, that's because something is up with him." Allison pushed a stray strand away from her face. "Then again, they are in the type of job that brings all kinds of stress."

Allison walked across the street back to her flower shop with the usual flair of a self-assured woman. Mindy lowered to a wooden bench she kept just outside her shop. It was a nice day, the sun shining brightly and the breeze was just enough.

Why did she feel so off? She had to not put so much stock in a man's attitude. It could be that perhaps Eric was just having a bad day.

CHAPTER FOUR

"CAN WE GET two glasses of Chardonnay, please?" Mimi's squeaky voice made Tori grimace. Why was the woman there again? Surely she had better things to do. Like perhaps convince Tobias to leave Montana.

Tori forced a smile at Mimi and her friend, a woman who'd used the wrong tone of self-tanner and was a very deep shade of orange. "Right away. Our special today is eggplant parmesan."

The women didn't reply, so she turned and walked away. Spotting Jessie, she motioned her over. "Can you take two glasses of Chardonnay to table five for me? I think I just threw up in my mouth."

Jessie laughed. "Either that woman loves Italian food, or she likes to torment you." The young woman tapped her temple. "If you give me her table, she'll know it's working."

"Ugh, you're right." Tori went to the small bar and placed two wine glasses atop the counter. She noticed both Mimi and the orange woman watching her. She forced a smile and whispered to Jessie, "I think you're right. She's here to annoy me."

When she returned to the table, Mimi threw a ten dollar bill on the table. "We won't be eating. If it takes this long just to get a glass of wine while you gossip, there's no telling how long a meal will be." She rolled her eyes and looked to her orange friend. "Come on, Ashley, let's go to the sandwich shop." Mimi slid out of the booth then grabbed her glass and took a long swig of her wine. "Oooh, a bit too tart."

Ashley didn't seem as convinced about leaving by the way she eyed the bread basket and then the wine. But she meekly followed behind Mimi.

Jessie came up and peered at the table. "Wow a whole ten dollars. Isn't the wine six dollars a glass?"

"Yep, but I came out ahead, she left." Tori huffed, picking up the glasses. "That woman is antagonizing me for a reason. Not sure what she's got to worry about since Tobias and I hate each other."

At ten that night, she locked the front doors to the restaurant and hitched a tote onto her shoulder. She still had a couple hours of accounting work to do. So there'd be no wine and television for her that night.

"Tori?" A man approached. Thanks to bright headlights, she couldn't make out his features, but being they shined directly at her, she was clear to him. Whoever he was.

"It's George Weston," he said, acknowledging she couldn't see much more than his outline.

"Oh, hey," she called back. "I heard you were going to be in town. Saw your mom at the grocery store last weekend."

She and George had dated for a few months right after college. He'd accepted a job in Helena and, being that their relationship was too young, she'd not been inclined to go with him.

"Yeah, I'm back for a bit. My parents are retiring and I'm here to help them clean out some stuff and help them with their accounts."

When he neared, she noted he'd not changed much. With sandy brown hair, blue eyes and an athletic build, George remained handsome. The only tell he was in his forties were the laugh lines at the edges of his eyes.

He pulled her into an embrace. "I've been looking forward to seeing you. First night out since I got here. So I went over to the pool hall with Eric and Ernest."

"You and those two used to be like peas in a pod," Tori replied, genuinely happy to see George.

He tugged at her hair, a gesture he'd done while they dated. The action seemed a bit too personal to Tori, but she decided perhaps it was just something he did. "When can I spend time and catch up with you, pretty lady?"

"I happen to know this local Italian eatery that has the best spaghetti in town. How about lunch tomorrow? My treat."

He chuckled. "Can't take a day off spur of the moment, huh?"

"Not this week. It's Laurel Creek Founder's Week."

She pointed to a banner that had been stretched across the main road. "Yours truly is in charge of raffle ticket sales. And you're spending money on some tickets, Mr. Weston. There are some amazing prizes going to be given away."

She smiled up at him, enjoying the sparkle in his eyes. "So lunch and tickets is all I can offer this week."

"I'll walk you home. Still live at the cottage over there?" He motioned with his right hand and with his left, took her elbow. Although the action wasn't intimate per se, it made her distinctly aware of how long it had been since she'd dated.

They walked to the door of her cottage, which was just down the block and across the street. He looked at the front door and then to her. "This place suits you perfectly. It's small and very cute."

"Thanks?" She smiled coyly. "See you around then?"

"Yeah," he replied and, once again, hugged her. Tori cleared her throat at the sudden urge to cry. What the hell was wrong with her hormones that a simple hug from a man made her want to cry?

She went inside and leaned on the closed door. If she wasn't careful, she and George would making out. Being he was only there for a short time, she didn't want to enter into anything that would only make her feel even lonelier when he left.

The cell phone rang and she dug into her purse. It was Allison.

"Did I just see a man walk you home?"

Tori laughed. "What is wrong with you? You are about to get married, why aren't you having sex or something? Seriously, I didn't peg you for a Peeping Tom." She walked to the side window and peered out to see the Allison's silhouette at her upstairs window. Allison waved.

"I was looking out to see if Taylor's truck was parked yet. He's gone to a call and, as usual, I'm worried someone's going to shoot him."

Tori couldn't imagine. "Stop fretting. It's probably the nerds over at the pool hall. They always get into an argument at closing time."

"Yeah, you're right." Allison paused. "So who was that?"

"Remember George Weston?"

"The hot track runner you dated after college?"

"That's the one. He's in town for a bit to help his parents with some projects."

Allison whistled. "And is one of his projects Tori?"

It was hard not to laugh at the truth in Allison's statement. "He may think so, but it's a no. I am not about to jump into a temporary fling. I want to date someone who is stable, plans to stick around and make it permanent."

"You've turned down every guy that has asked you out lately."

Tori nodded. "Yeah, but that's because I wasn't ready. I'm ready now. I may actually go back through the guys that remain available and see if anyone is still interested."

"Wow, you are serious." Allison clicked her tongue. "I'll have to help you. You're bad at choosing men."

"I beg your pardon," Tori pretended to be offended. "Need I reminder you of Icky Ted? That guy you dated was so gross."

"He had kind eyes."

"And dirty hair, stinky breath and long fingernails."

"Eww, yes, he was gross," Allison said then gasped. "Oh, I have to go, Taylor's here."

The call ended and Tori stared back to the now empty window. "Good night, Allison."

LEAH LIFTED HER wine glass and took a tentative sip. She'd not tried that particular brand before and, although the aroma was good, she hated when wine turned out to be bitter. She was pleasantly surprised to find it was well rounded and substantial in flavor.

"Yum."

"Thanks." Luke, her hunky man, walked into the kitchen from the hallway wearing only sweatpants and carrying his little dog, who looked over to Leah as if she were an interloper in the relationship. Leah wanted to laugh.

"I was referring to my wine. Although I have to admit, you are a yummy sight." Truth. His muscular build never ceased to amaze her. The man had an amazing body and being he was drop dead gorgeous didn't hurt one bit. It still boggled her mind that he was all hers.

She scowled and met his gaze. "I have a problem. You need to help me."

"I'll get you a snack," he told the dog, placing the little runt down on the couch. He gave her his full attention while digging in a cookie jar for a dog biscuit. "What's wrong?"

Leah took another sip of wine. "Mimi wants me to throw her a bachelorette party. Me, the woman who has only two close friends, is supposed to plan a party. And need I mention that both of my friends don't like her?"

True to form, Luke just lifted his eyebrows and slid a look to his dog that'd been joined by hers. The dogs watched him with expectation and he went over and gave them their treats. "You can always go with her and do one of those woman things…nails or whatever." He walked back to her and hugged her.

"Nails?" Leah laughed and pressed a kiss to the center of his chest. "Thanks, Babe."

She let out a sigh. "I suppose I can plan a girls' night out and invite Allison and Mindy. Allison has to come since she's family and Mindy is sort of dating Eric, so she'll also feel obligated."

Luke was content to nod.

"But then I feel bad not including Tori. Not that she'd come anyway, but still. This is such a huge mistake. You really need to talk to your brother."

"Tried. He didn't want to hear it." He pressed his

lips to the side of her neck and began licking at the sensitive spot. Leah squirmed and tried to get out of his embrace. But when he nipped at the skin, she couldn't help but moan. "My brother is as stubborn as I am and he doesn't want to hear it. Made up his mind."

"That is so crazy. Why is he getting married?"

Instead of a reply, he lifted her up into his arms. "Let's finish this conversation in the bedroom."

"You know darned well we won't be talking in there."

"But you may come up with a good idea of what to do."

"No, I won't. My brain is already fuzzy."

CHAPTER FIVE

T HE RAFFLE STAND was just outside Victoria's. Tori, joined by Helen, one of the festival planning committee members, stood beside it selling tickets and enjoying the festivities. Tori wore her usual dark pants and green polo shirt with "Victoria's" embroidered on the left side of her chest. She felt frumpy next to Helen who wore a crisp white blouse, red floral skirt, perfect makeup and, of course, she had bright red nails that matched her skirt. Helen always looked ready to attend a soiree of some sort.

"We are doing brisk business," Helen announced. "Today is the relay race. I love watching the teams come together and participate in this. Did you hear the Hamiltons are competing? Brothers and cousins."

She hadn't. "No, I didn't know but, then again, they compete every year."

The wind blew Helen's perfectly coiffed bob and she patted it into place. "Tobias, Luke, Ernest and Eric are running. Taylor is the coach." Helen giggled. "Eye candy day."

"Should be interesting." She looked to the start line where people were congregating. It would also be the finish line. "Looks like most of the town are beginning to show up."

Tori peeked at the program. The race was to take place in an hour. She would find busy work in the restaurant so she wouldn't have to deal with Tobias. No doubt, Mimi would be around bouncing and ensuring everyone knew they were engaged. As if the whole town didn't already know.

"Oh, here comes Tobias now," Helen announced. Sure enough, her nightmare swaggered across the street toward them. Why the hell was he coming to where she stood? He'd been giving her a wide berth lately. But then again, he did enjoy antagonizing her. He wore a loose, unzipped sweatshirt over a tank top and running shorts that showed off his well-sculpted legs. She'd always liked his legs.

"Ladies," he greeted. "I've been sent to fetch Miss Romano."

"What for?" Tori scowled. "You planning to get me run over as I cross the street?"

He studied her with the lazy look of a man too bored to speak. "Good idea." He shrugged. "Maybe later, right now I imagine Allison would kill me if I let you get hit by a car. Besides, you may not have noticed but..." he looked up and down the street. "Traffic is blocked on Main Street."

Of course, she'd not thought before speaking. Damn him for pointing out the obvious. "Who sent you?"

"Allison, I just told you. When you go get a personality transplant, ask them to throw in a hearing aid."

She almost laughed at his quip, but somehow managed to glare at him. "I'll have to remember not to ask you for a referral, because yours didn't work."

"Allison needs to talk to you pronto." He made a shooing motion and then went to stand next to Helen. "You look lovely today, Mrs. Sanders."

Helen blushed prettily. "Thank you, Tobias."

Tori hurried to where Allison stood holding a basket of items. Her friend looked overwhelmed and gave her a concerned look. "I need your help, I'm desperate." She shoved the basket, which held numbers and pins, into Tori's hands.

"What's the matter?" Tori asked.

"I just got a call from a customer. She's on her way to pick up a bridal party flower order. I thought she wasn't coming until the morning. I have to finish packing it up. Can you please go pin numbers on the runners?"

She gave Allison a droll look. "Sure go ahead. Although I am not sure why the runners need stupid numbers."

Allison giggled. "It's so they feel more athletic, I guess. Remember that whole conversation? You were there at the committee meeting when it was decided and, if I remember correctly, you thought it was a splendid idea at the time."

"That was before I realized the dumbass was going to be one of the runners," Tori mumbled, walking to the start line.

Each team had a different color patch and they were numbered one through four for the relay. There were to be two runs and then the best of the two would run for first place the following day.

The mayor was in the center of the square talking into the microphone. He was rambling on about one of the raffle prizes and encouraging people to buy tickets. One prize was a weekend at his hunting lodge. Tori wondered if whoever won would be more interested in a getaway by the lake than actually hunting.

She began sorting the team members, finding out the order and then helped pin a number on the front and back of each shirt.

When it was the Hamilton Team's turn, she fortified herself. "Keep it together, Tori. Don't stab him."

Luke was first. The ever-present scowl softened somewhat when she approached. He'd be first. She pinned a blue number one on his shirt. Leah stood by chatting about something or other. Tori looked around her to see if Mimi was there. But surprisingly, the only woman present was Leah.

Next she pinned Ernest, who would be the second runner. Eric was third and Tobias was missing.

Taylor turned to her. "Have you seen my cousin?"

"He was over talking to Helen last time I saw him."

Taylor didn't respond. Instead, he called the other

three over to talk. Tori shrugged. Tobias could run without a number, she really didn't care. She went to the next team and pinned their numbers on and then headed back toward her restaurant and ticket table. She'd have a good view of the race from there.

"I need my number," Tobias snapped, cutting off her progress. "Number four. The one who's gonna cross the finish line first."

She couldn't think of a retort. "Stand still." She handed him the numbers and put the basket down. "Take your sweatshirt off."

When he lifted a brow, she grabbed the numbers back. "Hurry up, the race is about to start."

He shrugged off the sweatshirt revealing a tight blue tank top.

When she rounded him to pin the number on his back, immediately the thought of his bare, wide back made her hands tremble just a bit. She'd loved running her hand down the wide expanse of skin. The taut muscles bunched when she touched him.

After hurriedly pinning the number, she went to his front. "Don't move, it's too tempting to stab you."

His lips curved, but he remained quiet and very still.

Under his close perusal, not only did her hands shake but also it became hard to breathe. Damn her stupid body that would always be affected by the idiot. Finally, the job was done.

"There, all done. You best hurry on over to the start line."

He took one of her hands, not letting her move away, and looked into her eyes as if searching for something.

"You will always be the one that I can't let go. For that, I hate you."

With those words, he pressed a kiss to her palm and then stalked away.

Tori remained rooted to the spot, a sensation like that of a boulder on her chest wouldn't let her take a full breath.

"I hate you, too, Tobias. I hate you so very much," she whispered.

"We still on for lunch?" George shook her from her thoughts. "I'm looking forward to Italian."

"Sure." Tori was glad for the distraction. "Come on, let's watch the race from over here." They went to the ticket stand. The few people gathered there were all looking to the gazebo where the mayor was now introducing the teams.

When he mentioned the Hamiltons, what seemed like a chorus of women shrieked. The Hamiltons all lifted their arms in greeting. The next team was introduced, which included several local horse trainers. They would be the strongest contenders against the Hamiltons. Each team was then told they had to have a woman when it was discovered the third team, a group from the pool hall, had one woman running.

Tori laughed as the teams scrambled. Leah was recruited for the Hamiltons' team and poor Mindy was dragged from in front of the coffee shop to run for the horse trainers.

"I'm surprised you didn't get recruited," George told her with a chuckle.

"I'm short and they probably figure I'll get overtaken easily."

Soon, a horn blew and the runners took off. Luke was just ahead of Frank, one of the horse trainers, when rounding the corner and handing off to Ernest. Before long, Tori was cheering just as loudly as everyone else when Mindy and Leah raced. Leah had long legs and had always been quick. She reached Tobias ahead of Mindy who lost speed at the end. Tobias exploded out of the start line, everyone let out a collective cheer. He ran so fast that it was obvious the horse trainers' team member would not be able to catch up.

When Tobias rounded the corner and broke through the finish line, it was a full minute before the next competitor came through.

As the racers all began high-fiving and celebrating, the mayor began announcements for the second race.

"I see your ex just won," Helen commented, not seeming to notice George was with her. "He's such a great guy."

Tori cleared her throat and looked at Helen. "The team won Helen, not just Tobias."

"It was pretty close until he got the baton," Helen insisted.

Great, now they were going to have a conversation

about her ex-fiancé in front of George. Not that it mattered. She wasn't planning a relationship. But what if she was? Small towns were annoying.

George laughed at something Helen said. Tori had been too busy being annoyed to hear what she'd said.

"What did you say?" Tori asked the woman whose eyes twinkled with mirth.

Helen looked to George. "I was telling George about how the constant banter between you and Tobias is always rather entertaining. Everyone knows you really don't hate each other."

"Oh, I definitely do not like the man," Tori said with emphasis. Just then, runners rushed past and both George and Helen stopped paying her any mind. Tori let out a breath.

The ending to the second race was a lot closer.

Allison hurried over and hugged Tori. "My client just left with the bridal order. I'm so bummed to have missed the relay races. Thankfully, I don't have any clients expected to stop by tomorrow, so I shouldn't miss anything else today."

She stopped talking and looked up to George. "I'm sorry, here I am babbling on and on. How are you, George? Long time." George beamed at Allison and accepted her hug. She pulled back and studied him. "What have you been up to? Married yet?"

Tori hadn't thought to ask if he was married. Of course it made sense, most of the people she'd been to high school with were either married or divorced. There were few like her that had never married.

"I am married and have three kids. My family is still in Helena. My wife is a physician and is reluctant to relocate. So I'll probably end up living there forever. I'm going back as soon as I get all this work done at my parents' place." He motioned to Tori. "Hey, Tori and I are about to have lunch and catch up. Why don't you join us?"

Feeling like an idiot, Tori met Allison's gaze. "Come on, Allison, let's catch up."

Together, they went inside. The dim interior was not only cool compared to the sunny day, but also the aroma of herbs and cheese was always welcoming.

"I can't believe it. The smell of good cooking brings back all kinds of memories." George walked in a circle sniffing the air.

Tori nudged Allison. "Married," she whispered.

"Sorry," Allison replied softly.

"Don't be," Tori insisted. "I didn't have any expectations."

"Good." Allison nudged her back and spoke in a louder tone. "Why don't we sit in a booth by the window so we can keep an eye on the goings-on?"

They had a perfect view of the town square where the race participants and spectators mingled. Tobias leaned on this truck, talking to the horse trainers' team when Mimi came into view.

Allison rolled her eyes and quickly picked up her drink when George gave her a curious look. Of course, they were in the perfect position to watch the blonde wrap herself around Tobias and kiss him as if she were auditioning for a porn flick.

It took monumental effort not to gag. Instead, Tori touched her foot to Allison's then motioned to George with her head. The man was practically drooling at the view of Mimi's ass pointed in their direction.

"So, George, what does your wife look like?" Allison asked and Tori choked on her breadstick.

BOOM. BOOM.

Tori narrowed her eyes toward the front of the restaurant. She was almost done closing up. This was not the time for "one last meal" request.

"We're closed!" she called out from behind the bar where she was finishing putting up clean glasses.

Boom. Boom.

"Damn it," she mumbled. Since there was always the possibility it was an emergency, she went to the door and yanked the door open only to become more annoyed. Why didn't she check before opening?

Tobias walked in. "We've been calling you and you didn't answer your phone."

She narrowed her eyes at him. "Who's been calling me? I usually have my phone on silent while I'm working."

"Allison, Taylor...we're all at their house."

This time, she glared at him. "So why are you the

one here to fetch me? They really don't want me to come otherwise they would have sent someone I like."

He looked up at the ceiling and let out a breath. "Come or don't. I really don't give a shit."

Dressed in lose sweats, no doubt over the running outfit, he reminded her of how he used to dress after a track meet in high school.

It was hard to keep from laughing, so Tori gave up. "Wow, you are the perfect example of a welcome party."

Tori walked behind the bar. "I'll stop by for a moment." When he didn't move, she pinned him with a raised eyebrow look. "Don't wait. I can make it the short way from here."

"Who was that guy you were with earlier?"

Before she could stop herself, Tori rushed closer and shoved him. Unfortunately, he was too big and didn't budge an inch. "None of your business. Why would you even ask?"

"I can ask. You don't have to answer." He shrugged. "Just curious, making sure you're okay."

"Okay?" She hated that her voice pitched into a strange squeak. "It's not your place, Tobias."

He took her arm and brought her closer. "It could've been, but you messed it up."

"For fuck's sake. It's been twenty years. When are you going to let it drop? I broke up with you. It's been well established I was a bitch. Let's move on."

And, of course, her throat seized up and her eyes welled. Why in the hell was she so emotional all of a sudden? He'd moved on. Tobias was engaged. It was her who hadn't moved on, could barely keep a relationship.

"I'm sorry." He released her. "You're right. I need to stop bringing it up." When he noticed her shiny eyes, his widened. "Ah shit, did I make you cry?"

"No. I'm not crying." Of course, a stupid tear rolled down her cheek. "I'm fine. Tell Allison I'll stop by tomorrow."

He didn't move. Instead, he hugged her and pressed a kiss to the top of her head. "I'm an asshole."

She had to turn her head to breathe, which meant her cheek was against his chest. "I'm broken, Tobias. It's me who's got a problem. I've never been able to make a relationship work. I can't seem to commit to anything other than this place."

Patting her back awkwardly, he then lifted her chin so she could look up at him. "You're not broken, Tori. Just particular."

A chuckle escaped. If anyone looked through the window, they'd be shocked to see the two people who constantly fought in an embrace.

Tori looked away. "I'm ready to close up. If you release me, I can step back and finish up."

It took her breath when he pressed a kiss to the tip of her nose. "So who was that guy?"

"Oh my God!" Tori pushed away. "You can only be human for short spurts."

"I don't see why it's so hard to answer," he replied, following close behind her. "Just tell me who the guy was."

"Augh?" Once again Tori's voice hitched. "It was George Weston. You know George from high school."

"Oh, yeah, George." Tobias cocked his head to the side and stared at her. "How long have you two been dating?"

She rounded him and went toward the door and held it open. "You have to walk outside so I can lock up."

"Is your boyfriend still in town? Does he know you'll dump him when the going gets tough?"

Tori charged him and punched him in the nose. It felt as if every bone in her hand broke. Stars appeared behind her eyes, and she hopped in a circle. "Ouch. Ouch. Ouch."

When she looked over at him, she let out a scream. Tobias held both hands up to his nose, which didn't stop the blood from seeping through his fingers.

"Why are you bleeding?" she yelled. "I think I broke my hand."

"Get me damned towel." Tobias grabbed the closest tablecloth sending a vase and salt and pepper shakers flying. He slammed the cloth to his nose and let his head fall back.

"What is going on?" Allison stood at the door with Mimi behind him.

Tori groaned. "He ran into my fist while saying something stupid."

"Sweetheart?" Mimi screeched, running to Tobias and attempting to pull his head lower. "What did she do to you?"

Tobias grunted and stalked around the three of them, dragging the tablecloth behind.

"He may need some ice. I need ice for my hand," Tori said and went back inside. Just when she took a step, Mimi jumped in the way to block her.

By the snarl, narrowed eyes and flare of her nostrils, the woman was about to explode. "I am so sick and tired that every time I turn around you're throwing yourself at my fiancé. Why don't you get it in your thick head? Tobias is over you."

A good friend to the end, Allison attempted to intercede. "Mimi, you're mistaken. Tori does her best to stay away from Tobias. Besides, they always fight."

"They fight because she's always up in his face," Mimi insisted, not taking her eyes from Tori.

Tori wasn't about to take the woman's crap. If the furious woman tried to hit her, she was going to lose it. "Get out of my restaurant. I don't throw myself at Tobias. You need to talk to him, not me, about boundaries."

"What is that supposed to mean?" Mimi leaned forward and pointed a finger in Tori's face.

Tori slapped her hand away, immediately regretting it when pain reminded her of why she needed ice. "You need to leave now," Tori gritted the words out past clenched teeth.

"And if I don't."

"Oh my God. This is ridiculous. I am not about to

fight over some idiot."

There was shuffling behind her. Taylor walked in and looked to Mimi and then to Tori who was cradling her hand against her chest. "Mimi, you need to go see about Tobias. His nose might be broken."

Tori's eyes rounded, but she didn't say anything.

Thankfully, Mimi left after giving her one last glare.

"Maybe I should take you to the clinic," Allison said. "Your hand is swelling."

"Why is this happening?" Tori sank into a chair. "We're in our forties. Why is some guy's girlfriend in my face? We left high school twenty years ago."

"Try over twenty," Taylor quipped.

"Let's go." Allison patted Tori's shoulder. "We better get that looked at."

Tori nodded and looked at Taylor. "Is Tobias going to press charges?"

"Nope, said he deserved it."

HER HAND WASN'T broken, but it was badly bruised. After wrapping it in an Ace bandage and recommending over the counter pain medication, she was sent home. In the waiting room, she was annoyed to find Mimi sitting with Allison. The blonde pretended not to notice Tori, which suited her just fine.

"I'll take Tori home. See you later," Allison said to a morose Mimi. "Call if you guys need anything."

Once outside, Allison let out a long breath. "She is

such a bitch. Taylor said she yelled at Tobias the entire way to the clinic. Now, she's demanding they move to Billings immediately."

"He's the one that wants to marry her. Should have taken time to know her first." Tori couldn't help but wonder what would happen to the Hamilton land and the effect on the family if he left. Tobias was an idiot for all of this. If he loved Mimi, he had a strange way of showing it.

Allison waited until they were on their way back to the center of town before she began to talk. It was only a ten-minute drive to the clinic, so Tori couldn't allow herself the luxury of pretending to sleep.

"Tori, you need to step back and look at the obvious. Tobias is coming to you because he wants you to talk him out of getting married."

Her heart skipped all over itself and Tori held out her left hand. "Oh, no. Don't go down that road. Everyone's tried to talk sense into him. Luke, Taylor, Eric, and even Ernest. If Luke can't talk him out of getting married, what makes you think I can do it?"

"You're our last hope." Allison sniffed. "They've asked me to talk to you for weeks, but I agreed with you. It's his stupid choice...and well..."

"Well what?" Tori kept an eye on the road. Allison was an emotional person and she wasn't in the mood to get into a car wreck. No more injuries for her.

Once again, Allison sniffed. "I see now what Taylor tried to tell me. You and Tobias. You have a lot of anger and resentment to get through. The reason neither of you have been able to form a good, stable relationship is because you're ruined. You ruined each other."

Ruined.

She repeated it and the word stuck in her throat and she fought to keep from gasping for breath. So she kept silent, unbending even when Allison asked her to say something.

Finally, when arriving at her house, she practically jumped from the car.

"Thank you for the ride, Allison. I'll talk to you tomorrow...or the day after. I'll probably stay in bed tomorrow." She walked into her house, locked the door and went directly to bed.

The sooner she fell asleep, the faster she could pretend none of this had ever happened.

CHAPTER SIX

NOT ONE TO be waylaid by a broken nose, Tobias broke through the finish line tape the following day to help his team win first place in the Founder's Week relay. Although his nose made it a bit uncomfortable, the adrenaline of running made him forget about it for a few minutes.

After lingering for a couple hours and enjoying some of the festivities, he got home to begin preparations for the week ahead. Thankfully, the labs, Duke and Scamp, were exhausted after a day in town, so they immediately sought out their dog beds and were asleep within minutes.

He had to admit the quiet of the house was welcoming and he wondered how different it would be once he and Mimi married. After the entire debacle with Tori, now she was even more demanding about moving to Billings.

The first thing he had to take care of the following week was to speak to Luke and Taylor. All three owned the ranch and had to make a decision together about what to do.

After pouring a tall glass of ice water, he went to his favorite chair and fell back into it. It had been a long day and now it was time for painkillers, water and some mindless television watching.

The doorbell rang and Tobias groaned. "Who the hell can it be now?" He glanced toward the dogs. They didn't bother to wake up.

"Fine. I'll open the door and get murdered. You two just rest," he muttered as he trudged to the door.

He was probably asleep and dreaming. That was the only explanation as to why a beautiful woman dressed in a flowing summer dress that didn't require a bra was standing just outside.

"Tori?" He squinted at her. "What are you doing here?"

Her chest lifted when she took a deep breath. "I came to talk to you. We have some things to clear up."

True statement. But so much left unsaid never made them actually have a discussion before. He took a step back and motioned with his hand for her to walk inside. When she walked into the house, her perfume, a light, sweet scent, tickled his nose. Damn she smelled as good as she looked.

Her short hair was tussled and there was some sort of sheer color on her lips. Tori had always been the kind of woman that was naturally beautiful and rarely wore a lot of makeup. She didn't have to.

Her gaze met his and she frowned. "You've got a black eye. I did that, didn't I?"

"Yeah, you pack a heck of a right hook." He went to where he'd been sitting. "Sit down. This talk sounds like something serious."

When he sat, she squeezed into the wide recliner right next to him. The sides of their legs touched which, of course, sent all kinds of awareness through his body. Tori, on the other hand, seemed too distraught to notice.

"Tobias, I owe you a huge apology." Tori covered his hand with both of hers. "There is never any excuse for striking someone. I couldn't sleep a wink last night and, all day, I've been on edge. I had to come and apologize to you." Her eyes filled with tears that threatened to spill over.

He lost the ability to speak and just stared at her.

Tori took another fortifying breath. "I can't believe I hit you. You've been an asshole and super annoying, but you've never put your hands on me in a way that would cause any harm. I don't know what came over me that I did that. Please forgive me."

It wasn't anything to take lightly. If he was to be honest, her striking him had hurt his feelings. Although there'd always been animosity between them, they'd never pushed each other to the point of actual rage.

"I pushed it. I kept goading you until I got a reaction. I accept your apology and, believe me, I know this is not in your nature." He smiled at her. "I owe you an apology for my part."

She shook her head. "We don't like each other. We fight. It's our thing." Her lips curved, making a piece of his heart melt. However, he wouldn't be so stupid to ever allow her into any part of his heart again.

"We've got a thing?" He lifted an eyebrow, his gaze moving to her lips. "I didn't know."

Although she shifted, Tori didn't move away. "I'm serious. I wanted to talk about the way we get along and how crazy it is to always be arguing. But Allison told me you're moving after you and…" she looked away.

Tobias cleared his throat. "Yeah, she wants to live in Billings. Especially after what happened yesterday."

She met his gaze for a prolonged period. Seeming to search for an answer of some sort and not finding it.

WHY IN THE hell had she let Allison talk her into this? She'd finally agreed to speak to Tobias about his decision to marry. Words got jumbled in her brain, every sentence rewriting itself before she could utter it. "About that. Why are you getting married?"

There was a flicker in his gaze, but then he assumed the usual annoyed expression. "The reason everyone does. To settle down and start the second phase of a relationship."

"That sounds rehearsed." She removed her hand from over his and swept hair that didn't need to be moved to behind her ear.

He took a loud breath as if finding It was surprising

that he'd been holding it and looked at the television screen. "We are all either going to get married or remain single. I've decided I don't want to be alone forever, so I'm getting married."

"So you're just going to marry her? Allison said you admit to not loving Mimi."

Tori held her breath, expecting that any minute Tobias would explode. He would set her in her place and none-too-gently show her out the door.

When he stood, she forced her gaze to trail up his legs, past his flat stomach and broad chest to meet his darkened eyes. "Stand up."

"I'm trying to have a civil conversation with you. Ensure you don't make the biggest mistake of your life."

His arm wrapped around her waist and the second under her legs. Tori yelped when he lifted her up into his arms. "Yeah, about that."

Her mouth fell open, absolutely not one word forming when he stalked toward his bedroom.

IF THERE WAS a way to close her eyes tighter, Tori would've done it. She didn't want to dare hope that they were going to end up in his bedroom. In his bed.

The air sizzled, sparks igniting so bright and constant, she wondered if it was all just a cruel hoax of her imagination. Any moment now, Tobias would nudge her and make a crude comment.

But it didn't happen. When she opened her eyes to

meet his breathtaking hazel ones, their gazes clashed like angry ocean waves against jagged rocks.

It was inevitable that she pull him down for a kiss. The hunger would not be denied.

Their time, their way.

If she had been interrogated before this day, Tori would have admitted that the only way for them, for her and Tobias, to ever clear things up between them was that they would have to connect. It would take raw, uncensored sex and emotion to purge years of anger and frustration.

There were so many things to apologize for. So many lost occasions, events and memories that they'd pushed away and ignored.

The moment fell over them like lightning and their kiss became raw and hungry, this was not the time for pretense. She accepted his tongue fully and deeply into her mouth, allowing barely a second before tangling with her own in a desperate dance that sent her body into tremors of want.

How she needed him.

"Take your clothes off." Tori tugged at his shirt, her nails clawing into the fabric. "I want you now."

Other than a groan of agreement, he remained quiet. Immediately, Tori was transported back to when they were engaged. They were so young. She was only eighteen and he twenty-two. Even then, their lovemaking had always been raw and urgent. He'd rarely spoken during it, while she'd recited entire Shakespearean works.

Her dress was done away with, the flimsy thing lying on the floor in a graceful pool of white and flowers.

His sweatpants, shorts and briefs made a less elegant pile.

"Don't say anything other than 'Fuck yeah'," Tobias said, his mouth next to her ear as he trailed light bites down the side of her neck.

Trembling with need, Tori could barely stand. Seeming to sense it, Tobias cupped her bottom and lifted her to wrap her legs around his waist. His thick erection prodded at just the right spot and she ground into him. The friction of their bodies gave more than took and before long, she was losing control.

"Damn it, you have to fuck me or I'm going to scream," Tori said, taking his mouth once again with hers while she ran her hands down his back and up to rake her fingers through his hair.

They fell onto the bed and he didn't waste a moment. Thrusting into her with force just the way she'd always liked it. It had to start off hard and fast. She preferred getting off right off the bat before building to a second climax.

Suddenly everything went still. Both of them realizing what they were on the brink of doing. "Shit." Tobias slid to the side of the bed and sat with his legs over the side. "Shit," he repeated.

Tori was sat up, her body trembling at the realization they'd been on the brink of making love. "Damn it," she said sliding to the opposite side. They sat without moving facing away, each in their own thoughts.

"I came here to talk. I'm not leaving until we do." Tori was proud of herself. She wasn't going to be the first one to acknowledge how they felt about each other. That conversation would be too painful.

She had never stopped loving him and by the way they'd just connected, neither had he. However, it was one thing to love someone and another to forgive them.

"God, Tori, there's nothing to talk about. If my family thinks you can talk me out of something, they must have all done some sort of strange drug."

She turned and studied his profile. Damn the man was gorgeous. He'd become more handsome over the years. "I think it was a combination of meth and cocaine."

"Did you think you could actually change my mind?" He slid a look at her. "I suppose if anyone can, it's you."

Whatever it meant, it made her catch her breath. "All they want is for you to be happy. Between Taylor and Luke, there has been so much sadness and loss in their lives that they want to protect you from it."

"I'm not a child. I can protect myself." This time when he looked at her, there was a clear message.

Tori nodded. "You're right. I have yet to be forgiven for what I did. And it's been what, twenty years?"

"I would if I could, but I can't."

She reached over and touched his shoulder, enjoying the feel of his warm skin. "Be sure you're doing this for the right reason and with the right person."

After the awkward way they'd stopped, when she slipped from the bed, she felt exposed and hurried to dress, rushing from the room immediately.

The house was quiet; the only sounds were the two dogs snoring in their beds. One of them, Scamp, lifted its head and gave a soft bark of acknowledgement.

She had already grabbed her small purse when Tobias came out of the bedroom. He'd pulled on his sweatpants.

With tussled hair and a bare chest, he was breathtakingly tempting. "Be careful driving back."

"Like you care. If I wrapped my car around a tree, you'd probably have a barbecue to celebrate."

The edges of his lips twitched as he understood what she was doing. "Yeah, I'd get out my guitar and play, *Ding Dong the Witch is Dead.*"

"Kiss my ass." Tori went to the door and yanked it open.

"Been there, done that."

She huffed and closed the door firmly behind her.

Tori drove about a mile down the road before she was forced to pull over. Sobs racked her body. He was going to get married. Tobias Hamilton was going to move and would be gone from her life forever.

CHAPTER SEVEN

I T WAS A windy day, which meant Mindy had to hold down her skirt with both hands as she made her way to Eric's front door. This was quite bold of her, but after a week of being ignored, it was time to find out what the problem between them was.

Just like a man to avoid a situation instead of just talking it out. Although she was emotionally invested and already cared for him, that didn't mean she wasn't realistic. Sometimes situations changed.

Circumstances and feelings changed all the time and there wasn't anything that could be done about it. However, being they lived in a small town and would be seeing each other regularly, it was best not to have it be an awkward thing.

Eric lived two streets over from main on a quiet side street. His house was an unassuming one-story ranch house with a garage and a very well-maintained front lawn.

She knocked three times and then put her arm

straight down in an attempt to keep her A-line skirt from blowing up and exposing her rear to the world.

Wearing a tank top and sweats, Eric opened the door. His eyes narrowed at first against the brightness of the sun and then widened upon seeing her.

"Hey. Come in." He moved back and ran a hand through his hair. "Sorry, I wasn't expecting company."

She noticed there were socks on the floor next to the couch and an open magazine, but other than that, the room was neat.

"I was about to pour myself a glass of soda. Do you want some?" He motioned to the kitchen.

So far, he didn't act awkward. A bit surprised she'd stop by, but other than that, he seemed relaxed. Interesting. "Sure, I'll take a Coke if you have one."

"What brings you to my door, pretty lady?" he asked, placing a filled glass of soda on the counter next to where she stood.

She cleared her throat. "Why have you been avoiding me?"

Eric was tall and muscular, a striking physique that seemed to run in the Hamilton family. Every one of them, even Ernest, who was more the athletic build, had amazing bodies. She'd met Luke and Tobias' sister once and, although svelte, she, too, was blessed with an amazing body.

While he seemed to ponder her question, Mindy allowed her gaze to linger on his chest. Eric was a quiet guy, shy and reserved. But he seemed at ease with her since they'd been on several dates, one where their make-out session had become quite ardent.

"I need a clear head to make a decision." His gaze met hers for an instant. "It's hard to think straight when I'm around you. All I want to do is kiss you."

Her heart skipped. So his feelings hadn't changed. However, he didn't seem at all happy at the moment. "What are you trying to decide?"

If he told her he might be gay, she would drive herself into a tree. His brother, Ernest, was gay and in a relationship with a really nice guy. Did that mean Eric was also homosexual? She couldn't compete against a man or provide what he needed in a partner, so it would be no contest there.

"I was offered an opportunity for a position in Billings. It would be a promotion. I'd have to move."

Then again, she couldn't compete against an entire city or a better position either.

"Oh. Well that's good news. It means they hold you in high regard." She tried her best to sound peppy, but her tone remained flat. "Have you made a decision yet?"

Eric shook his head. "No. There's a lot to consider. Someone would have to replace me here. My family is here and you. You're here."

"Me?" Heat filled her cheeks. "I don't want to stand in the way of your career. We can always visit." The last word came out as a whisper. Their relationship was much too new to survive long distance and they both knew it.

"Visit?" His lips twitched. "Is that what you propose?"

Eric closed the distance between them and with fingers under her chin, lifted her face. "I don't want to visit." He lowered and covered her mouth with his. Mindy could've cried at the feel of him against her as she clutched his shoulders.

She fell against him as he encircled her waist.

The feel of him brought so many sensations, Mindy could have sworn the room tilted. Parting her lips for his tongue, she couldn't help but let a content sound escape.

He was like no other, broad, well-built and a great kisser.

"I want you, Mindy," he whispered in her ear. "Can I make love to you?"

Mindy responded by pressing harder against him. "Yes."

He took her hand and led her to the bedroom. It was definitely a man's room. The bed was unmade and clothes were strewn about. There was no art on the walls, and other than the bed and two night stands, there was only a dresser.

Mindy didn't care. All she wanted was to be with Eric.

They undressed quickly, each looking at the other and inspecting each area revealed. Eric's gaze bored into hers and then roamed down her nude body. It felt as if he touched each spot his eyes landed.

"You're perfect," he said, moving closer. She had just

thought the same thing about his body, but wasn't able to speak as his mouth covered hers.

They fell onto the bed, a tangle of limbs, and he came over her, never breaking the kiss.

Although Mindy was anxious to have him inside her, she also wanted the moment to last. Lazily, she slid her hands down his broad back, enjoying the sensation of his skin under her palms.

Eric didn't hold back when she wrapped her legs around his slender waist, he thrust in. The thickness of his erection filled her completely and it was all Mindy could do to keep from climaxing. Digging her nails into his back, she lifted her hips to match his drives, taking and giving in time.

They continued making love, nothing existing but each other.

THE AROMA OF spices would have normally made Tori inhale deeply and smile, but this morning, she wanted to throw up. Had she really done it? Almost had sex with Tobias?

After all the years of maintaining the type of relationship that guaranteed they'd not like each other, twice they'd allowed passion to overtake all reason.

Her temples thudded and her mouth felt as if she'd stuffed it full of cotton. After returning home, she'd drunk an entire bottle of wine and then started on a second one. Now she was paying a price for two dumb things.

"Good afternoon," Jessie called out with a bright smile. "You look like crap."

"Thanks," Tori said and trudged to the coffee station. "I feel like it, too. Someone slammed my head against every wall in my house and then poured sand in my mouth."

"Wine or liquor?" Jessie asked, holding up a bottle of aspirin. "Either way, we've got it covered, you need to take a couple of these, have a bowl of minestrone and go sleep it off."

True, she wasn't going to be any good the way she was feeling and sleeping would provide a respite from having to think about what she'd done.

"Yeah. I'll just check with Marco and see if he needs anything."

"He just went to the market, won't be back for an hour."

Tori lifted the dark coffee and drank it down. Although a bit too hot, she didn't feel a need to care. "I'm going home. Call me if anything comes up."

THE DINGS OF her cell phone woke her and Tori opened her eyes slowly. First one and then the other. No thudding, and although a bit thirsty, her mouth wasn't as dry. She peeked at the display to find it was already three in the afternoon.

It had been a long time since she'd slept a day away. The text was from Tobias.

Last night didn't change things
If anything, it proved that I need to do this
I'm still getting married.

She stared at the display and typed back.

Last night was truly a mistake
I don't care what you do

It was tempting to add the word dumbass, but she refrained. If the idiot wanted to make a mistake and end up with a second divorce, that was his choice. From now on, she'd stay out of any Hamilton issues. She wasn't part of the family and although his mother tried to keep her in the loop, it was time to cut that tie.

She slid from the bed and went to the shower. The hot water cascading over her skin helped wash away the night of bad choices. Once done, she hurried to the bedroom and pulled on clothes; jeans and a simple t-shirt. She slid on some tennis shoes and then dug in her drawer and pulled out the engagement ring.

With a small drawstring bag tucked safely in her purse, she went out.

THE HAMILTONS' HOME near Billings was welcoming. As soon as Mrs. Hamilton opened the door, her face brightened and she smiled warmly at Tori.

"I'm so glad to see you, come in." Tobias' mother was a pretty woman who always reminded Tori of being a teenager. When she started dating Tobias, she'd often spent afternoons in their kitchen. Mrs. Hamilton and her mother had been good friends and often visited each other.

Although it was nice, it made it hard to sneak off with Tobias to make out. The mothers always kept vigilant eyes, claiming they would not allow the teens to ruin their good friendship.

In the end, it had not ruined it, but made the two women closer.

"What brings you to town?" Mrs. Hamilton said, leading her to the back porch. "I was out here watering the plants and watching the hummingbirds."

"Oh my goodness," Tori exclaimed at noticing the four feeders. All of them had tiny birds fluttering around them. "How cute. Look at that one. Oh, over here, there are three of them."

For a few moments, she allowed the whimsy of the moment to allow her to relax. While Mrs. Hamilton watered the plants, they talked about what was going on at Laurel Creek. Tori filled her in on the relay races and finally admitted to punching Tobias on the nose.

"He probably deserved it," Mrs. Hamilton said with a shake of her head. "That boy has always spouted off without thinking."

Tori met her gaze. "I apologized to him. There is

never any good reason to strike another person."

Mrs. Hamilton laughed. "You obviously didn't grow up with boys. They punch and kick each other regularly. Even nowadays, they fight like boys in a schoolyard over every little thing. A few months ago, Luke and Ernest had a fist fight and then the twins are always giving each other a black eye or a busted lip."

At Tori's wide gaze, she added, "However, you are right. This is different."

"He's still planning to get married, Mrs. Hamilton. He told me so. So, I've decided to return the ring so you can give it to him to give to Mimi."

"That's not going to happen. I am not giving that woman the ring. I may just have it reset and gift it to Clara," Mrs. Hamilton said, referring to her daughter. She took the proffered bag and placed it on a tabletop.

It was best not to interfere and ask why. Her heart was already broken at the decision to distance herself from the Hamiltons.

Mrs. Hamilton studied her for a moment. "What about you? It's time for you to find a good guy and settle down."

"I'm not sure I'll ever find someone that I want to sacrifice my independence to," Tori replied with a chuckle. "I like not sharing a bed."

"I can certainly understand that," Mrs. Hamilton said. "Especially with these Hamilton men. They are so bulky."

Tori looked away, not wanting to think about the

fact she'd shared a bed with a Hamilton just recently.

When a hand pressed down on her shoulder, she wanted to lean into the kind woman and cry. "You'll always have us. I consider myself your aunt. Look at me."

It was not what she wanted. This was going all wrong. How to tell her she'd decided to part ways, to not stay in touch?

The kindness in the woman's eyes chipped at Tori's resolve. "You have been part of our lives since you were a kid. Don't let the fact things didn't work our between you and Tobias and that he's getting married change anything. Promise me."

Shit.

Tori let out a long breath. "I will be in touch and even come visit when it's safe. But I don't think it's a good idea for you to continue to invite me to family gatherings. Mimi is already demanding they move away from Laurel Creek because of me. I don't want to cause any more problems."

Mrs. Hamilton's face hardened and she shook her head. "That boy only learns when he goes headfirst into a big mistake. But there's nothing to change his mind." Her expression suddenly changed and she dug a cell phone out of the front pocket of her pants. Holding up a finger, she dialed a number.

"Hi, Sweetheart. I'm fine. Did you get a chance to make any inquiries?"

There was a long pause as she listened to whomever she'd called. Then her eyes widened. "You should speak to my son about this."

Again she listened and rolled her eyes. "Well, you tried. I'll call him…or no, I think I'll go visit the dork myself."

She hung up and her lips curved. "Sorry about that. I remembered I had sent Eric on an errand. If I don't call about things when I recall them, they can be lost forever."

They laughed at the comment and although Mrs. Hamilton seemed to be at ease, something about the phone call was strange. For some reason, Tori felt as if it had something to do with her, or would affect her in some way.

Since Mrs. Hamilton didn't offer any explanation, she tried to figure out a way to find out which son she'd spoken about. "Is Luke in some kind of trouble?"

"Oh, goodness no. Leah has been a godsend. My Luke has been improving steadily. He still goes to see a counselor on a weekly basis, mind you, but the improvement in him mostly has to do with Leah."

Tori was genuinely glad to hear it. "That's great. They make a great couple."

"Yes, they do," Mrs. Hamilton said, studying her. "So do Allison and Taylor. Now to find you a Mr. Wonderful."

What was it about parents and their relentless desire to match people up? "Don't suggest Eric. He's infatuated with Mindy, the woman who owns the coffee shop."

"I heard," Mrs. Hamilton said. "He's got a job offer

to move. I think to either Helena or Billings, I forget. Anyway, if he takes it, I'm not sure how it will affect those two."

Her heart broke for Mindy. "I wonder if he's told her yet. I don't want to break the news if he hasn't."

"I certainly hope so." Mrs. Hamilton picked up the watering can and began to water the plants again. "Did you know, my nephew, Alex, is moving to Laurel Creek? He's divorced. Tobias invited him to come out to the ranch, get a fresh start."

"No, no, no," Tori held up her hands as if stopping traffic. "Don't even think about saying anything to this Alex about me. I am not interested in dating any Hamilton."

Mrs. Hamilton laughed. "Tobias ruined you."

BEFORE HEADING BACK to Laurel Creek, Tori went shopping and then treated herself to an expensive meal. The day turned out quite lovely. If she were to be honest, it was a great distraction from what awaited at Laurel Creek.

There was the restaurant to deal with. Marco had spoken to her about becoming a partner and was more than prepared to help more with the business aspect. She needed to hire another server or two as they had discussed expanding to the empty space next door.

With the money from the partnership, Tori could pay for her portion of the expansion and then treat herself to a trip to Hawaii.

Things were moving in a good direction business-wise. As far as her personal life, that was a different story. She decided to join a dating website and start dating. It was time to live. As far as Tobias, she could possibly speak to him about keeping their distance.

Nah, it was probably just best to ignore him until he got the hint.

A song came on the car radio and she cranked the volume up. As she sang with the song, a weight lifted from her shoulders. It was time to take control of the future, not worry about the things she couldn't control.

She was single, had good friends and a thriving business. The only thing missing was a dog. Her lips curved as she headed to the local shelter, which was actually a small ranch on the outskirts of Laurel Creek, where a couple fostered animals.

CHAPTER EIGHT

MINDY COULDN'T BELIEVE it. After years of not dating and months of tension between her and Eric, he was leaving. He'd not confirmed it but, in her gut, she could feel the separation between them.

He'd been more than gracious when she'd gone over to his place. Had chatted and they'd made love, but there was definitely a wall.

The bell over the door rang and for two days now, each time, her stomach flipped. It wasn't Eric.

Taylor, the town's sheriff, walked in. His muscular build seeming to shrink the interior of her shop. He stopped at a table and spoke to a couple of women and then came to the counter.

His hazel gaze met hers for a moment before moving to the espresso machine. "I need extra caffeine in my coffee today." Lips curving into a smile made it obvious why he did. Obviously he and Allison had enjoyed each other's company.

"Got it, extra shot of espresso," Mindy said, returning the smile. "Muffin to go with that?"

She always gave the police officers a free pastry. There were only four on the force and, to her, it was a way to show her appreciation. "They are fresh."

He nodded. "I could never turn that down. Oh, and can you give me a coffee to go for my cousin?"

Mindy laughed. "Which one are you talking about?"

"Eric." He let out a breath. "He's stuck working on paperwork all day."

The statement made her sad, she'd looked forward to seeing him. She turned and began making the beverages. "He told me about the job offer."

"What do you think?"

"Sounds like a good opportunity for him."

"If that's what he wants."

The whirl of the espresso machine gave Mindy an opportunity to collect her thoughts. She poured the dark liquid into a portable coffee cup and carefully placed a cover on it.

When she turned, thankfully, the urge to cry had passed. "It almost sounds like you're not sure it's the best thing for him."

Taylor frowned. "You are correct. It's not all about work. There are always more important things." He picked up the cup carrier and the bag with two muffins and gave her a crooked grin. "Thanks."

The rest of the morning went quickly and at three in the afternoon, Mindy was ready to head home for the day. Her afternoon employee always arrived at three and would remain until closing. She went outside, deciding to walk to Allison's flower shop and chat before going home to an empty house.

In the afternoons, Mindy went to a yoga studio twice a week and then once a week she and several ladies met for coffee. This day, however, she was free, normally one of the days when she cleaned or shopped for groceries.

Mindy trotted up the steps to the front door of the flower shop. Instead of the tinkle of a bell, Allison's door had a chime and three musical notes sounded.

Tori was sitting next to Allison and both women turned with wide-eyed looks of people who'd been conspiring. Once realizing it was her, they visibly relaxed.

"What are you two up to?" Mindy neared and plopped down into a chair. "You look guilty about something."

Allison tossed her wild curls behind her shoulders. "We are plotting how to escape for a day to Billings. You should come with us."

"Why do you have to plot?" Mindy asked perplexed.

"Because we don't want to invite Leah," Tori said. "We want to shop for her birthday. But if she finds out we went without her, her feelings will get hurt."

"If we both close shop and go, people will talk. It shouldn't be so damned hard to get away," Mindy said.

Allison chuckled. "Small towns make life hard. What if we ask Luke to make plans with her for the day? So even if you invite her, she'll say no."

Tori, who sat in a plush chair, pulled her legs up and hugged them to her chest. "Thought of that, but he'll screw it up. Besides, I wouldn't put it past her to tell him they'll do it another day just to go with us."

A customer entered and Allison went to help them. Tori looked to Mindy. "Are you okay? I heard about Eric's possible transfer."

"I'm not okay. But I will be."

Tori nodded. "I'm sorry. It sucks."

"Yes, it does."

THE SUN SETTING made it hard to see and Tobias squinted against it. Country music blasted from the radio and the air whipped into the cabin of his truck. A long drive normally settled his mind and gave him a chance to be alone with his thoughts.

Ever since the night he'd almost made love to Tori, he'd not been able to concentrate on shit. Every single moment of that night replayed in his mind over and over again. As soon as he woke up, she was there, the picture of her under him. Her breasts perfectly positioned for him to suckle.

Damn, he was doing it again. Where the hell did he put his sunglasses?

The good thing about living in Montana was the opportunity for long drives with no distractions but the slopes and valleys of the landscape. He pulled down the visor and it helped a bit with the glare of the sun. It was too late now, but he should have headed east so not to have the annoyance of the sun in his face.

A song came on the radio and he began to sing along. Damn if he didn't sound good. Tobias chuckled and began singing again. Tori and he had a song. Whenever Boys II Men came on the radio, Tori would shriek and force him to slow dance with her. He'd acted annoyed but, secretly, he had loved any chance to hold her close. Damn, she'd felt so good against him. No one else ever came close to that. She was his one. And damn it, he was man enough to admit it. Just like he was man enough to know he would never fully trust her.

The sound of a horn jarred him to reality, but too late to respond correctly. Tobias cranked the steering wheel to the right. But he turned it much too sharply. He realized the mistake when the truck careened out of control.

It wasn't clear if the vehicle rolled or slid on its side. Metal against metal grinded and something cut into his left leg. The music continued to play. It was too loud. Suddenly, the truck came to a stop, hitting something so hard his upper body flew forward and his face smashing into something.

And then a thick fog fell. A groan sounded. Tobias wasn't sure who made the guttural sound. Maybe him. The smell of automotive liquids and smoke burned his nose and he struggled against the tightness pushing in his chest.

This was not the time to pass out.

"No."

Darkness fell.

CHAPTER NINE

ANXIETY WAS REAL. Tori felt tingles of awareness sweep through her and she did her best to push it away. "I need some lavender tea," she said, more to herself as she made her way to where Allison kept a beautifully decorated tea area in the flower shop.

Enchanted Garden was the most Zen place Tori knew. With the perfect ambiance of soft music, flowers, a gurgling fountain and the aroma of tea brewing, a person had no choice but to relax.

And yet, her body was strung tighter than a guitar string.

"Something wrong?" Allison gave her a puzzled look. "You look on edge."

Mindy had left, heading to the grocery store, so they were alone again. "I have no reason to feel anxious and yet I do. Maybe I need to go to the gym and sit in the sauna for a couple hours."

"That's about an hour and a half too long," Allison said with a grin. "You never make it past fifteen minutes.

"You're right. I hate the heat." Tori poured the hot water and went back to the round table set in the back of the flower shop. "I'll drink this. It will make me relax."

The chimes sounded as Taylor stormed in with a thunderous expression. He raced up the stairs and came back down at a sprint. "I forgot my damned keys."

He went to Allison and kissed her forehead. "Meet me at the hospital. Tobias has been in an accident. Sounds bad."

In a flash, he was outside and, minutes later, the siren sounded.

Both Allison and Tori sat frozen. Neither said a word for a few moments. It seemed as if everything swirled around Tori, the entire room swaying and going in and out of focus. Allison must have been having a similar reaction because she remained without moving as well.

"Oh my God," Allison finally said. "Someone has to tell Luke. In a way that won't have him ripping off to the hospital and ending up in a wreck himself."

Tori nodded, hearing only every other word. "I bet Eric is heading to the scene. That only leaves us and maybe Ernest to break the news."

"Shit. Come on." Allison grabbed Tori's hand, tugging her to the door. She flipped the sign on the door to "Closed" and locked it. "I'll drive. You talk to me so I don't lose control. We need to go to Ernest's office and then head to the hospital. Hopefully, Taylor will call me with updates."

Hamilton Law Offices was located two streets over in

a one-story building. The receptionist must have seen something in their expressions because she didn't bother to try to stop them from going straight to Ernest's office.

The attorney sat in a corner chair. There were papers strewn all over his desk and on the floor. He held a folder and flipped it closed when they walked in. His expression of surprise quickly changed to concern. "What's wrong?"

"Tobias was in an accident. Taylor said it sounds bad," Allison started wiping tears.

Ernest immediately jumped to his feet.

"We're headed to the hospital," Allison continued. "I'm hoping you can break the news to Luke. No telling how he'll react."

Shadows of concern marred his handsome face. "Yeah. I'll do it. Shit. Do you know what happened?"

"Hold on." Allison dug her cell phone out and pushed a button.

"Any news?" she asked and then listened.

"Mmm hmmm."

She ended the call. "A trucker was on the scene. Apparently, Tobias veered into the oncoming traffic lane and then lost control. The ambulance is there now. They're extricating him from the truck."

There were a couple beats of silence before Ernest went to his desk and opened a drawer. He grabbed his wallet and keys and motioned for them to exit before him.

"I'll see you at the hospital."

LUKE WATCHED AS two calves circled playfully and he pushed his baseball cap down to keep the glare at bay. The end of a day was always his favorite part. Not today, however. He'd been restless and not able to focus. Hopefully, it didn't mean he would have another flashback or some shit.

He dismounted and released the horse to graze. If spending time out in the wide open, being married to a damned-near perfect woman and surrounded by family didn't fix him, nothing would.

Admittedly, things were better. The episodes were far apart and although it sucked, he couldn't really complain. It sure beat how horribly things were headed just a couple years earlier.

His cell phone buzzed. It was tempting to let it go to voicemail and not worry about it. If the call was important, they'd leave a message. When it buzzed the third time, he pulled it from his shirt pocket and looked at the display.

The picture of Leah's face always brought lightness to his chest. She was his salve, the only prescription he really needed.

Before he could say anything, she spoke. "Come to the house. Ernest's here."

His annoying cousin. The one who he wanted to punch every time they saw each other. What the hell was Ernest doing there?

"I'll be there in a minute." He ended the call, suddenly filled with urgency.

Moments later, he released a still-saddled horse into a corral and hurried to the house. Ernest met him outside. Unlike the usually scowl upon seeing him, his cousin seemed more cautious as if gauging his mood.

Yeah, so he was like a volcano, lava always brewing just under the surface. But did the asshole have to act like he was a wild bear not to be fucked with? Luke almost chuckled. Then again, it was good that Ernest was not exactly at ease around him.

"What?" Luke said, nearing. "Someone steal your panties and you think it was me?"

"I didn't know you wore panties," Ernest snapped.

Leah peered from the doorway. "Don't start. This isn't the time." Her worry-filled gaze met his, making his heart sink.

"What happened? It's Tobias, isn't it?" Automatically, he knew and not waiting for Ernest to say anything, he ran into the house to find his truck keys.

"I'll drive," Leah said.

"What the fuck happened to my brother?" Luke glared at Ernest who followed them out the front door.

"Car accident. When I left the office, they were extricating him from the truck. Ambulance was there."

"You're coming with us, asshole." Luke didn't want to hear any excuses and he wasn't quite sure why he wanted Ernest there in the truck with them. Then again, of course he did. If for some reason he lost it, Ernest would keep Leah safe.

"I can drive," he said, gently taking Leah by the shoulders. "Please."

"What if you lose control? Sweetheart, let either me or Ernie drive."

He met his cousin's gaze. Yeah, so they fought like two bulls, but he was family and the Hamiltons always stuck together.

"Let's go in mine, the engine's running," Ernest said without inflection.

"Fine."

"I'll call your parents," Leah said as they climbed into Ernest's SUV.

The drive was excruciatingly long. Every mile seemed to stretch to three. Leah spoke to his parents in low tones, ensuring to keep her voice calm to not alarm them more. She didn't say anything about the fact Tobias had to be cut out of the truck. Instead, she just said he'd lost control and was heading to the hospital to be checked out.

She tapped Luke's shoulder. "Your Dad."

"We're heading there now. Call me as soon as you get to the hospital and give us an update," his father said without preamble.

"I will," Luke replied, a lump forming in his throat. In the silence, he knew what his father was expecting. As identical twins, he and Tobias had an uncanny connection that to this day still puzzled him. "He's gonna be fine, Dad," Luke finally said.

There was another silence. "Good," his father finally said. "Luke?"

"Yes?"

"I need you to keep it together, Son. Need you to be there for your brother and for us. You hear me?"

"Yes, sir." He ended the call, his eyes stinging. "Damn it, why is it taking so long to get there?"

Ernest sped up. They were already way over the speed limit but, at this point, all they cared about was getting to the damned hospital.

Leah's phone rang and he realized it was still in his hand. "It's Allison," he said to his wife and passed the phone back to her.

The road ahead seemed to melt away and his vision blurred. Luke shook his head and he blinked several times. It was hard to focus, but he couldn't lose control. Not today.

CHAPTER TEN

W HEN LUKE WALKED into the waiting room, every
eye turned. Tori jumped to her feet and rushed
to him. Not as an attempt to stop any reaction from him,
but because she'd known him and Tobias since child-
hood.

"He was rushed to surgery," she said, touching his
lower arm.

Luke's gaze bored into hers. The look was so lethal,
she almost took a step backward. There was no reaction
and he didn't respond.

Seeming to sense the dark place her husband was
headed, Leah placed a gentle hand on his shoulder. "Let's
see if a doctor can give us an update."

Tori walked alongside as they went to the area where
a nurse stood talking to Taylor.

The nurse looked up as they neared, her gaze narrow-
ing on Luke. "You're the brother." Her voice remained
calm, without inflection. She didn't wait for anyone to
give Luke any details. It was as if she instinctively

understood he needed to hear any news directly from her.

"Your brother has sustained head trauma. There is a brain bleed that must be stopped, which is what the surgery is for. He's broken his left leg and right wrist. There wasn't any time to assess any other injuries. So far as we know, there could be some internal bleeding, but not enough to be worrisome at this point."

She waited, allowing Luke to digest the information. Tori had to take shallow breaths. She was having trouble imagining Tobias, who was so strong, being in a life-threatening condition.

"How long has my brother been in surgery?"

"They just went in," the nurse replied. "I will return as soon as there's any news."

No one moved as the doors closed behind her. Finally, Leah stepped back and motioned for Tori to follow. "He needs to be left alone for a few moments," she whispered, the entire time keeping an eye on her silent husband.

Taylor, Ernest and Allison stood quietly speaking about who would talk to Luke and Tobias' parents upon their imminent arrival.

Tori didn't listen any further. Instead, she lowered to a chair by a window. Seconds later, a loud sob echoed.

Dressed in screaming yellow, Mimi dashed into the waiting room, her blonde hair in a high ponytail. She wore tight leggings, tank top and matching running shoes.

Rushing to Luke, Mimi almost grabbed him when Taylor half-tackled her away. "Not a good idea," he said, pulling her to where Leah and Allison were. "They'll fill you in."

By this time, Mimi was making strange sounds. "Ah. Ah. Ah. What happened to Tobias? Is it bad? Ah. Ah. Ah."

Thankfully, Mimi was too deep in the throes of despair to notice her, so Tori remained seated. She eyed the exit and wondered if she could make it out without Mimi seeing her. Of course, in the hurry to get there, she'd left her purse in Allison's car. The only thing she had with her was her phone.

"You're staying," Eric said, lowering to sit next to her. "That woman has the most annoying cry," he mumbled, rubbing the bridge of his nose.

A cup of water was poured and shoved into Mimi's hand. She was aided to sit. The entire time, she continued to make the strange sounds. If not for the situation, Tori would have rolled her eyes and told her to shut up.

Leah went to Luke and spoke to him in low tones. He'd not moved from the same spot. Still like a statue, it was interesting to watch his body relax after a long moment. Finally, he allowed Leah to guide him to sit down, but not too far from where the nurse had walked out. His gaze remained locked to the door.

Tori's heart broke for him. So much had happened to him, it would be a travesty of justice for his twin to die. At the thought, a sob got caught in her throat and she gulped it away, not wanting to draw any attention to herself. The nurse had said Tobias was suffering from a brain bleed. He was in the operating room having brain surgery.

How in the hell did this happen? Tobias wasn't the reckless type. If anything, she would have expected any of the other men in the room to get in a car accident before him. It was probable the truck driver was the one that crossed in front of him. That had to be it. Since Tobias was unconscious, the semi driver could have said anything to cover up his fault in the accident.

The waiting room doors opened and Tobias' parents hurried in. Behind them were Clara and her husband.

"Come, I'll fill you in." Taylor went to them, taking Mrs. Hamilton's hand in his. Her face was flushed and her eyes reddened and swollen. She rubbed a wrinkled handkerchief across the bottom of her eyes, focusing on Taylor. Mr. Hamilton held a hand on her back and they stood huddled with Eric joining them.

The family was listening intently as Taylor and Eric filled them in on what had happened. Mrs. Hamilton and her husband looked to Luke every once in a while with worried expressions. The poor couple had to worry about both sons in this instance.

There was very little conversation as the waiting continued. Mrs. Hamilton sat next to Luke, his hand clasped in hers. He'd not moved, continuing his vigil on the doors.

Clara sat next to Tori. "This is horrible. He has to be

okay." She sniffed and Tori squeezed her hand.

Eric returned to sit with Tori, his eyes constantly moving from the doorway to the others in the room.

"Were you one of the first on the scene?" Tori asked in a whisper.

He nodded. "Yeah, the fire department was already there. Tobias was unconscious."

There were so many questions, but Tori didn't want to say anything out loud that would give her answers she didn't want to hear. "Do you think he really swerved into the other lane?"

Eric nodded. "By the tread marks on the road, it was obvious he did."

They lapsed into silence for a while until Leah and Allison stood. "We're going to go get coffee," Allison said. "I preordered so we won't be but a minute. Going to the coffee shop across the street."

"No, you both should stay," Tori said. "I'll go. Family should stay."

Mimi gave her a droll look. She'd finally stopped crying and sat next to Mr. Hamilton. "That's a good idea. She should go." It was obvious she didn't mean just for coffee.

It wasn't the time for pettiness, so Tori ignored her.

"Thank you, sweetheart," Mrs. Hamilton said with a tenuous smile.

When she returned half an hour later, there hadn't been any news yet. Just as she sat, however, the doors opened and the same nurse walked out. Immediately, everyone got to their feet and rushed toward her.

Tori often wondered how medical professionals could maintain serenity in the face of so much travail. The nurse looked to each of them without expression. Other than seeming to be searching for the words to begin, she didn't give any indication of what the news was.

"Mr. Hamilton is out of surgery and in recovery. Everything went well. The doctors were able to assess the injuries and repair any damage. We will know more in twenty-four hours."

She waited for the words to sink in. "They went ahead and took care of the internal bleeding. The doctors had to remove his spleen."

"When can we see him?" Mrs. Hamilton asked. "Will he regain consciousness soon?"

The nurse shook her head. "Not for a bit. The doctors feel it's best to keep him asleep until the swelling fully goes down. Only two people would normally be allowed to see him tonight. In about an hour or so." She met Luke's gaze. "I'll make an exception so that you can see your brother."

Luke nodded. "Thank you."

"So when can I see him?" Mimi asked, not bothering to identify her relationship to Tobias. "I've been here for hours."

Everyone's reactions varied from flabbergasted to annoyed. The nurse, however, remained the consummate professional. "After the initial twenty-four hours, we will reassess, Miss."

Mimi huffed and went back to sit. "That's ridiculous."

When Eric shifted, Tori realized she's been hanging on to his arm, her fingers digging into it as if he were a lifeboat.

"Can we continue to get updates tonight?" Tori asked then clasped her lips tight. She'd not meant to ask, but since no one else did, she took it upon herself.

The nurse nodded. "Yes, I work the night shift. I will come out periodically to let you know of any changes." She motioned to a phone on a small desk. "You're welcome to pick up the phone and call the nurses station if you have any other questions. We will address any concerns you may have."

She left, promising to return for Luke and his parents and everyone went back to sitting and waiting.

"I'm sure he'll recover fine. He's strong and still relatively young," Eric told her, patting her back awkwardly.

The mood in the room didn't lighten. Although it was good news that Tobias had gotten through the surgery, there was still the fact he'd be kept unconscious.

Leah stretched. "I'm going to go home to shower and put on some sweats. I'll bring back a couple pillows and blankets."

"Good idea," Allison said. "I'll do the same and bring back some snacks." She looked to Tori. "Want to come with me?"

Tori shook her head. She couldn't fathom moving in that moment. Things could change without notice. "No, I'll stay."

Understanding, Allison nodded. "All right. I'll bring you back a blanket and a pillow."

"Thank you."

Mimi jerked around. "I'll go with Leah."

"Maybe you should stay with Mom," Leah said, looking toward Mrs. Hamilton.

"No, go ahead," Mrs. Hamilton said. "I'll be going in to see Tobias and there's no telling how long that will be."

The three women left and Tori moved across from where Mrs. Hamilton sat. "Do you need anything?"

"Just to see my son. I want to see his face," Mrs. Hamilton said, her eyes moving to the doorway into the ward.

Mr. Hamilton met Tori's gaze. "Remember when you two got in a wreck in high school?"

"Yes. That was so scary."

He smiled. "He hit a tree to avoid hitting a damned cat," Mr. Hamilton said, shaking his head. "Totaled my car."

Taylor spoke up next. "I hit that same tree months later."

"That's when I took a chainsaw to it," Mr. Hamilton said with a chuckle.

Tori blinked away tears as she noticed his eyes misting.

THE EXTERIOR SET of doors opened and Mindy rushed in with bags and a drink container. She greeted them and then went to a side table to set up, pulling muffins from the bag and then setting up disposable cups.

Eric tried his best not to show how glad he was to see her. But damn, she was just what he needed.

He stood and went to her. "Thank you for this," he said and she gave him a soft smile.

"It's the least I can do."

Her eyes met his for a second before she went to his aunt and Tori, expressing her support. The women talked for a few minutes as he watched from across the room.

In times like these, he got comfort from knowing that if something ever happened to him, his family would be there. There was no question in his mind, they'd move heaven and earth to ensure he was well taken care of.

His parents were headed there and would arrive any moment. They'd waited for someone to come dogsit because they planned to stay the night there at the hospital.

It was what family was about. His anyway.

Finally, the conversation lulled and Mindy stood. She gave both the elder Hamiltons a hug and then went to Eric.

"I know this is a difficult time. I just want you to know, I'm praying for Tobias."

He took her elbow and guided her to the chairs.

"Stay for a bit."

Mindy met his gaze. "I can't, I have to open the shop for a group that's meeting there tonight."

He guided her out to a short corridor. "I would walk you to your car but, any moment now, he'll be out of recovery and, hopefully, we'll get an update," he said, looking over his shoulder at the doors.

"Of course. Please stay." Her gaze searched his. "Let me know if you need anything."

Eric nodded and, without thinking, he pulled her close and hugged her tightly. "Thank you."

When her arms circled his waist, every emotion inside threatened to burst and he let out a long, shaky breath.

"Your Kevlar vest is crushing my boobs," she whispered with a smile.

"Oh, sorry." Eric loosened his hold on her. Then without thinking, he pressed his lips to hers, enjoying the feel of his woman.

Mindy responded, but cut the kiss short at the ding of the elevator doors about to open. "I'll see you soon," she said and hurried inside.

CHAPTER ELEVEN

TORI TIPTOED INTO Tobias' hospital room. He was asleep, his face turned toward the door. His left arm was across his midsection, tubes connected to it. The other arm was in a cast from the elbow down to his hand.

Thankfully, he seemed pain free, his expression relaxed. There was a beeping sound from a monitor and his brow marred with a slight frown, but then it smoothed out.

Mrs. Hamilton had asked that Tori keep an eye out while she went home to shower and change. Everyone else had gone home this day.

The doctors expected Tobias to remain in the hospital another few days. At first, after surgery, he'd been in intensive care for three days. Once he'd been moved from ICU to a regular room, he'd made remarkable progress.

There was a cast on his left leg from lower thigh to foot and it was elevated. His hospital gown didn't cover everything, so part of his bottom was exposed. She neared and tucked the blankets around him to hopefully provide warmth and modesty.

Tori allowed her gaze to roam across his broad chest as she searched for signs he was breathing normally.

"What are you staring at?" he mumbled groggily. "Trying to figure out where you can stab me and make it look like an accident?"

"It would be easier to smother you with a pillow," she replied with a smile. "Or I could always inject something into this." Tori pointed at the bag that was dripping into his vein.

Tobias' brow crinkled. "Where's Mom?"

"She went to shower and change. You're stuck with me until she gets back. Are you in pain? I can call a nurse."

He shook his head. "I hurt everywhere. They'll bring me a shot of something in a bit." It was endearing when he frowned and looked at the IV bag. "I do need a drink."

Tori went to the nurses station and asked for juice. The nurse on duty, a pretty Latina, gave her a wide smile. "Your boyfriend is very handsome. He's a good patient."

She didn't bother correcting the nurse, too surprised to find out he'd not given the nurses any grief. Then again, they were probably bending over backward for the handsome guy.

"I'm surprised to hear that. He's normally a pain in

the butt."

The nurse laughed. "I'll bring him juice and a snack in a moment."

His eyes were closed when she returned, so Tori went to the window. It would be at least two hours before Mrs. Hamilton returned. There was a half-read book in her tote she planned to pull out and read but, at the moment, she felt too restless.

"I have an itch." Tobias said. "Right above my leg cast."

Tori came around the bed and lifted the blanket, doing her best to avoid lifting his gown. "Here?"

She scratched gently at the skin above the cast.

"Yeah." He closed his eyes with a pained expression. "Can you reach a bit around the back? Don't touch my ass. I know how you like my butt."

"Shut up." She did as he requested and stopped when he let out a sigh. "This is not going to be good. How the hell am I supposed to work?"

"Your Mom said she's taking you to her house. She and your fiancée will be closer to help out there."

He frowned. "Yeah, I don't think so."

"Oh, yes, you will," Tori said with one hand on her hip.

The nurse walked in. "Lover's spat?" She smiled at Tobias who grinned back.

Tori rolled her eyes and moved away as the nurse set up Tobias' lunch and juice on a rolling tray. She then checked his vitals and put a small cup with pills on the tray. "Take the medication with your juice, please."

He did as she instructed. She then rearranged his tubing so that it wouldn't tug and left.

"Why can't all women be as nice as Lydia?" Tobias said, looking to the door.

"It's her job to be nice to you," Tori said. "Plus, she doesn't know you."

"Where's Mimi?" He frowned at her. "Why are you here?"

It was so very tempting to pour the remaining juice over his head. "I have no idea. I'm here because I stopped to talk to your mom. She was tired and needed a break. Obviously, your fiancée wasn't available."

She glared at him for a long moment. "I'll leave as soon as your mother gets here. The only reason I don't leave now is because I promised to stay and watch you. She treats you like a child, which explains a lot."

Other than a one-shoulder shrug, Tobias didn't react to her statement. She dug out her book and read while he ate.

"I need to use the bathroom."

"I'm not helping you with that." Tori went to the bed and pushed the button. When the nurse's voice came over the intercom, she announced, "Your patient wants to poop."

"I didn't say that," Tobias argued. "That was uncalled for."

"You do though, don't you?" Tori grinned.

An hour later, they'd argued about several topics.

The chair was comfortable and if not for spatting with Tobias, she would have fallen asleep.

Her phone dinged. "Your mother is delayed. She fell asleep and just now woke up." Tori frowned at the phone. "I'm going to text Allison and Eric. Maybe one of them can come and watch her baby."

"I can be left alone," he said, but it wasn't convincing. It was obvious being in a hospital was affecting him. Tobias was normally fiercely independent. This needy side of him was nothing she'd ever experienced.

"You don't like hospitals." It was a statement, but when she uttered it, his gaze moved to hers and she saw fear. "Have you been hospitalized before?"

"No. I spent enough time in one when Luke was injured though." Tobias' hazel gaze moved over the room. "I hate the idea of a hospital. People come here to die."

Tori nodded. "We all have to go sometime."

"I know," Tobias replied. "I can't be here. It's too much like when Luke almost died. And those days after Taylor got shot. He was hospitalized forever."

"Yeah. You came home on leave for that." She remembered how no one expected Taylor to survive the multiple gunshots. "But you're okay and will be fine."

"I wish things were different," Tobias muttered and Tori instinctively knew they no longer spoke about hospitals and his injuries.

"They are what they are."

He lifted the cup of juice and drank through a straw.

"If I could change anything, I would change how much I fucking love you."

Tori's eyes flew wide and she inhaled sharply. "Don't say that. I don't want to hear that. You know damned well it won't solve anything."

Pushing a button, he positioned the bed so that he sat up straighter. "Do I? Will I ever understand how someone could dump a guy that heads out to war? Tell me one day you love me and the next its goodbye."

Nearing the bed, Tori lowered her voice to a whisper. "I begged you not to join the military. For days, I sobbed and pleaded that you stay with me. But you wouldn't hear it. You refused to listen to my fears and how much I needed you to stay."

"I had to go. My brother was gone and I couldn't handle that I wasn't with him. That he was in danger overseas while I stayed back."

Tori huffed. "What about me? You could just turn your back and leave me?" Her eyes misted as angry tears surfaced. "Did you even think about how it affected me?"

"What the fuck, Tori? You were here, safe at home. You had family and friends. You could've waited for me."

She gulped back a sob. "I couldn't handle it alone. I couldn't."

"That makes no damned sense. Why don't you just admit you were being a spoiled little brat?"

"Don't you call me that!" Her rage boiled just below

the surface. "You don't know anything."

There was fury in his gaze. Years of resentment shot at her. Tori figured it matched her own. "Why don't you enlighten me then?"

"You don't want to know. You really don't."

Tobias rolled his eyes. "What? That you had a nervous breakdown? I know about that. Mom told me."

"That's only the half of it."

Tobias pointed at her. "So it's all about you. How much you suffered. What the hell do you think I was doing? Vacationing in the sand?"

"I lost our baby."

No sooner did the words escape than Tori realized what she'd done. She stumbled backward and looked around desperately for her tote.

"What?" Tobias struggled as if trying to get out of the bed. Tori held both hands out. "Don't move. Stop. The last thing I need is for you to hurt yourself on my watch."

"What the fuck did you just say?"

"WHAT IS GOING on?" Mimi walked in and went directly to Tobias. She glared at Tori. "So now you come here to argue with him? Can't you just leave us alone?"

Tori and Tobias continued looking at each other. It was as if they were in a long tunnel, he on one side and she on the other end.

"I didn't mean to say that," Tori whispered.

Tobias looked at Mimi. "I need to talk to Tori. It's important."

"No," Tori interrupted. "Nothing can be done about it."

"Get out." Mimi spat in a low voice. "Get the fuck out."

Tori rushed from the room, sobs choking her as she raced to her car and the privacy it would offer.

CHAPTER TWELVE

TOBIAS WANTED TO break free of the bed and confinement of blankets and casts. The thudding of his heart was so loud he could barely hear Mimi going on about the scene she'd walked in on.

"I should have known. When I called your mother, she told me not to bother hurrying here until later. You have to talk to her and tell her that I'm more of a priority than Tori."

Her face was red and blotchy from anger. "I don't understand why your family hates me." The sounds of nose blowing made Tobias want to scream. Instead, he squeezed his eyes shut and pretended to fall asleep. Moments later, thanks to the drugs, he did just that.

When Tobias opened his eyes, it was dark outside. The room was serene with only one lamp lit. His mother sat in the corner chair where Tori had been. She had headphones on and was watching something humorous by the soft chuckles.

Upon noticing he was awake, she lowered the headphones to her neck. "Hello, sweetheart. How do you feel?"

Truth be told, for the first time in years, he wanted to cry. Mostly in frustration. Of all the damned times for Tori to drop a bombshell, She had picked the one instance when he could not chase her down and demand answers.

His mother stood and came closer. She pulled a smaller chair to his bedside and sat down. Then taking his hand in hers, she studied his face. "Tori called me. She is so very sorry about upsetting you at a time like this. I should have factored in that you two argue like cats and dogs before asking her to stay with you."

"Did you know about the baby?" He considered pulling his hand from hers, but decided to hear her out.

She nodded. "Not until it was over. Tori went to the hospital. Her mother told me it was because of a mental health issue. Then a year or so later, I learned what really happened. Tori's parents kept it secret, but her mother told me one day in confidence."

"Why didn't you tell me?"

"Because it would've been a burden you didn't need to carry. Especially not when you were overseas in a dangerous location."

Tobias hated that they acted like he was a damned war hero. His brother, Luke, was the hero. All he'd done was worked remotely from a safe distance. "It was my kid, Mom."

His mother nodded. "I know, sweetheart. She was

about five months along. It was a boy." Her lips curved. "I wish I would've seen him in person. But Tori has pictures and I saw them."

"Pictures," he repeated, not sure he wanted see them. His son had come and gone without him even knowing. Tobias swallowed.

"The doctors said she would have probably lost the baby anyway. The emotional upset didn't help. But, honey, you can't blame yourself in any way. Sometimes nature causes things that we cannot control." She took a shaky breath. "I'm so sorry, sweetheart." She wiped a tear from his cheek he'd not noticed, and pressed a kiss to the spot. "Do you need any pain medication?"

He shook his head. What he really wanted was to go back to sleep and wake up in his bed at home. This had to all be a dream.

The doctor entered, the white coat flapping against his thighs since the pockets were overstuffed with crap. He had graying temples, which gave Tobias some comfort. He hated when the damned doctors looked young enough to be his kid.

"Mr. Hamilton," the doctor greeted, reviewing his chart. "I hear you had an eventful day." He flipped the paper and frowned. Then he went to Tobias' bedside and leaned over, looking at his face. "The swelling is going down. I'm going to keep you here for another few days."

Tobias looked at the beeping machine at the same time the doctor studied it. "Doc, you said I could possibly leave tomorrow."

"No, I didn't." The doctor met his gaze. "I said we'd review your progress today. You've got a fever."

"What?" His mother stood and neared. "I didn't notice. But his cheeks are flushed now that you mention it."

"Mom, I want to go home. A fever is nothing to worry about, I'm sure." Tobias gave the doctor what he hoped was a triumphant look. Unfortunately, his eyelids felt heavy.

"Hey did you just put something in that?" Now his tongue felt as if it weighed a pound.

"Come and bring…" The doctor's voice faded.

What the hell was going on now? Tobias struggled to remain conscious, but quickly lost the battle.

IT HAD BEEN five weeks since his accident and Tobias wasn't sure he could endure another two weeks with the cast on. The only saving grace to not losing his mind was the fact his parents were entertaining to be around.

They'd settled into a routine that kept them quite busy and he enjoyed watching their playful banter over things from dinner choices to what to watch on television. It had been a long time since he'd laughed so hard when one night they decided to have game night.

Mimi came over often, but being it was obvious his mother hadn't warmed up to her as yet, she never stayed longer than an hour or two.

The ranch business worried him. He'd not been out there since he'd been released from the hospital. A soon as he got his cast removed, he was going home. Even thoughg his left leg was broken, the pain wouldn't affect his driving.

"What's got you so deep in thought?" His mother sat in her favorite chair and placed her cup of coffee on the table next to it. "A few more days and the cast comes off."

"And then the fun begins," he muttered. "Physical therapy."

She shrugged. "I'm sure you'll survive."

"There's so much to do at the ranch. I have to see about buying a new truck and also Mimi's pressuring me to set a new wedding date."

A frown marred his mother's face. "It made sense to postpone the wedding. You didn't feel up to wobbling up on crutches and I don't blame you."

"Yeah, I know, I understand why she's upset."

"Then tell her a month from now. You should be up to walking without aid, at least down the aisle."

Tobias shook his head. "We're not having a church wedding, Mom, I told you. We're going to Vegas."

"Oh, that's right. A tacky wedding."

He'd given up defending the choice to marry in Las Vegas. It was what Mimi wanted. He didn't care one way or the other. It was just a technicality in his opinion.

"What exactly do you plan to do once you get the cast off? You won't be able to do much at the ranch."

Thankfully Ernest and Henry were at his ranch helping out. So far, Ernst and Luke hadn't butted heads too much.

His cousin and his husband were troopers; Tobias was amazed at how supportive his family was through all of what had happened to him. "I'll ask Ernest and Henry to stay for a bit longer. Henry is really getting into the whole being a cowboy thing."

"You're fiancée hasn't been much help. I hope she makes a better wife than girlfriend," his mother muttered, getting up to answer her cell phone.

Tobias stared up at the ceiling. Maybe it wasn't worth it to bring Mimi into his "united" family. None of them agreed with this marriage. They would make her uncomfortable and that wasn't fair to her.

No, he'd made a commitment. He'd follow through and they'd live in Billings. That would be the only way to ensure this marriage worked.

He lifted his cell and dialed Mimi. "Hey. Let's do it in two weeks after I get my cast off. I get my cast off on Tuesday. We can go the following Monday."

Tobias listened to her counting off things she would pack and what she wanted to do after.

Finally noting his silence, she asked if he was sure.

"Yeah, I'm sure."

CHAPTER THIRTEEN

T ORI SIPPED HER wine and smiled. "I've lived in Laurel Creek my whole life. Except when I went away to college."

First date chatter was usually annoying, but she had to admit Allison had done a good job of setting her up with the handsome veterinarian from the next town over. His name was Alec, he was divorced and loved Italian food.

"How do you know Allison?" Tori asked when the conversation lulled.

He smiled. It was a nice smile. "We met at a dog funeral." He laughed. "It was nice to have someone there who found the situation as ludicrous as I did."

"I didn't even think about that," Tori said, attempting to keep a straight face. "I could have had a funeral for my doggie."

His eyebrows rose. "Seriously?"

It proved impossible not to laugh. "No, I'm kidding, but my dog did die recently. I am thinking of adopting another. I went to dog foster ranch, but they only had larger dogs, the smallest was medium sized and he didn't care for me at all."

"If you have a specific breed in mind, I can help. People drop off dogs at my clinic all the time."

Something shifted. Tori couldn't put her finger on it, but it felt as if someone was watching her. As discreetly as possible, she looked to the right and scanned the tables. Those that were seated were either engrossed in conversations or on their cell phones. One table of women was lifting glasses, toasting.

"Would you like more wine?" the server asked. Tori looked to Alec who smiled. "Sure, sounds good."

"I can't believe you're not attached," Alec said, taking her hand in his. "You're a beautiful woman."

A tingle traveled from their joined hands up her arm and she leaned forward. "Thank you. I'm always busy with my restaurant. But I've decided to take on a business partner and slow things down. Enjoy life more."

"I hope that means more dates," he replied and Tori was glad they'd hit it off.

Once again, she felt the sense of someone watching and she looked to her left. In the far corner were Mimi and a man Tori didn't recognize. Whoever it was sat back in his chair, one leg stretched out as if he were bored. It was strange for someone to go out to eat and act so oddly.

Mimi glared at her and turned away.

It definitely wasn't a date, neither Mimi nor the man

acted as if they wanted to be there. From the corner of her eye, she watched as the man flipped through papers and shook his head. Mimi pointed at something and seemed to get angry.

"Do you know them?" Alec asked, looking to where Mimi and the mystery man sat.

"I know her. Not exactly on friendly terms, but I find it strange that she's here having dinner when she lives in Billings." Tori decided it was best to change the subject. "How about you come to my restaurant next week? I think you'll like it."

The server came with their wine and Alec released her hand. "I'd love to."

"So how was the date?" The next day, Allison burst into the restaurant kitchen through the side door. "He's super cute isn't he?"

Tori had to smile. "Yes he is attractive and very easy to talk to. We made a second date."

"Oh, yay!" Allison jumped and clapped. "I'm so glad."

"Don't get too excited," Tori warned. "I do good on first and second dates and then I find excuses and suddenly get too busy to follow through."

Marco huffed. "Maybe you're scared of the sex part."

This was not a conversation she wanted to have with a man. Marco was in his late fifties and always bragging about his sex life. Obviously, his wife was well taken care of. Still, it was uncomfortable.

"I'm not scared of the sex part," Tori replied. "I think I have commitment phobia."

Jessie, who was rolling silverware into napkins, piped up. "I think with the right one, you'll jump into the mattress mambo, no problema."

Tori went to the side table and reached for tomatoes to chop. "Can we stop talking about my sex life please?"

"Why? I found it interesting." Tobias stood at the entryway wearing a t-shirt, jogging pants and a shit-eating grin.

As if a fire alarm pealed, the others scrambled out of the room, leaving them alone. Tori wanted to rush after them, but she'd have to go past Tobias and that was way too close for comfort.

"What the hell are you doing here? Aren't you supposed to be crippled or something?" She couldn't help but scan his body. He looked well, a bit thinner. No arm cast, only a brace, and he wore a black contraption on his left leg.

"Yeah, nice to see you, too." He hobbled to a stool and sat. "Good thing you're the only Italian restaurant, otherwise, your mouth would close the business down."

She knew everyone was just outside the door listening in. "What do you want?"

"We have a lot to talk about. I'm coming over tonight. Eight." He stood. "Oh, and you better be there."

"Bite me. I don't have to be anywhere."

He walked closer, until they were her nose to his

chest and glared down at her. Obviously aware the others were listening, he lowered his voice. "You can't drop the kind of news you did and just think it's going to stay at that. I want to see the pictures."

Her breath escaped and Tori fought to suck in air. "I can't…"

"Tonight." His gaze bored into hers. "I have a right…"

"Don't go there," Tori hissed.

Her hands trembled with anger as he left. Immediately, Allison rushed in. "Oh my God. You look pale. What was that all about?"

"He's such an ass," Tori offered as reply. "I'll see him tonight and after that, he won't ever want to speak to me again. The damned past is in the past. Nothing can change it."

Thankfully, an hour later, the awkwardness of the moment was gone. Jessie, a savior, shared about her husband's latest antics and had everyone laughing. Tori refused to allow Tobias to ruin her day. She finished food prep and then treated Marco and Jessie to a cappuccino and muffin from Cuppa Joe.

EVENING CAME TOO soon. Tori made sure the lights were on and she was dressed in baggy clothes with no makeup.

She'd asked Allison to call at eight thirty sharp to give her a reason to leave and ask Tobias to do the same.

On the dining table was a small box tied with a blue ribbon. She'd not looked in it in years, but often held it. Why had she been so stupid as to tell Tobias about the baby? Even if she wasn't on good terms with Tobias, she knew it wouldn't be easy to see the items in the box. Considering it, she went to the kitchen and retrieved a bottle of whiskey and two small glasses.

It wasn't quite eight when the doorbell rang.

Although she was prepared to see him, her body instantly reacted. Every inch of her being recognized him. How she hated how much Tobias affected her. His hazel gaze met hers, there was uncertainty and, for once, he didn't utter an insult or attempt to annoy her.

Instead, he just looked past her. "Can I come in?"

"Yeah." Tori moved back. She then walked ahead of him to the dining table. "Sit down." She busied herself pouring the whiskey into the short glasses.

"I can't drink. Still on drugs. No spleen."

"Oh," Tori said, pushing both away. "I forgot about your spleen being removed."

"Thank you, anyway. I'll take water though." His voice was tentative and low. Obviously, he was hoping to be prepared to see what the box held. He glanced at it, but didn't move to touch it.

When she returned with the glass, Tori decided it was best just to get it over with.

"I was about four months pregnant when I found out. I was scared and not sure what to do. It was too late to get an abortion, so I decided to tell you. That last night, we went out to eat and you got us a room at the hotel. Remember?"

"Yeah," he replied, his gaze moving from her to the box. "I remember."

Tori cleared her throat. "So anyway, when we got to the hotel, it had been so long since we'd been together that we didn't exactly talk. I expected you to notice, but you didn't say anything about my weight gain."

"I thought it was because you'd gone off to college and all. I didn't want to say anything because it didn't matter to me."

Tears stung and Tori closed her eyes, willing herself not to cry. She wasn't going to cry.

"Anyway," she continued. "You proposed and when I said yes. Just as I was going to tell you, you announced you'd joined the military and were going overseas. The moment didn't seem right at that point."

"Still you should have said something." Tobias' voice was hoarse. "I wish you would have told me then."

"I was too mad. You'd not discussed joining the military. We'd agreed that after my second year of college, we'd return to Laurel Creek. I would work at the restaurant and you would work for your uncle as an attorney."

His brow crinkled. "I'd forgotten about that. I did plan to be a lawyer, didn't I?"

"You did."

Tobias drank some water. "What happened after I left?"

"It's a blur. I told my parents about the baby. They wanted me to tell you immediately. But I kept putting it off. I was a dumb nineteen-year-old kid, who couldn't handle the stress of war. Soldiers were dying overseas. I became obsessed about it, was glued to the news twenty-four-seven. I had a mental breakdown and lost the baby at almost five months along."

With shaky breaths, Tori reached for a tissue and wiped at her eyes. "I blamed you, but it wasn't your fault. You didn't even know."

"That's why you broke off the engagement."

Tori nodded. "Yes. I was heartbroken. I wanted you with me, to go through the grief with me. It was unreasonable. I know that now."

She untied the ribbon and opened the box, pushing it to him. "His name is Thomas."

Tobias couldn't pull his eyes away from the picture. The baby seemed as if he were asleep. Perfectly formed with the serene look of an infant. He had dark hair and a dimple in the center of his chin. The Hamilton chin. His lips curved at noting that.

The tiny hands were curled into fists beside his face, the blue blanket surrounding him was like a cloud for the little angel. A tear trickled down his face and Tobias ignored it.

His son. A little boy who'd never had a chance. "Why did he not make it?"

"The doctor said it was just too soon. He needed more time." Tori was full out crying now, her reddened eyes blinking away the tears the spilled over. "I held him for hours. He was so very perfect and beautiful, Tobias."

"I can see that." Tobias looked to her. "He looks like both of us."

She sniffed and nodded. "He does."

"I'm so sorry," Tori said, taking his left hand in both of them. "Please forgive me for keeping this from you. It was horribly unfair of me. Your mother asked me several times over the years to tell you, but I guess it was too hard."

Her cell phone rang and she looked to the display. Tori answered. "Hey, Allison. Yes. Everything's fine. We'll talk tomorrow. Yes. I'm sure."

"Wants to make sure we're not choking each other?" Tobias said, attempting at lightness.

Tori smiled and wiped her eyes. "Yeah. She sounded shocked to not hear you screaming in the background."

They went through the rest of the items in the box. There was a stack of pictures, some of Thomas alone and a few with her and her mother holding him. Tobias asked for a few and Tori gave them to him.

The birth certificate, death certificate and several other items were also in the box. There was a small jeweler's box lastly and Tori handed it to Tobias. "I had this made for you, but was too chicken to ever give it to you."

It was a chain necklace. On the end was a small vial

with ashes. "His ashes," Tori said in a whisper. "You don't have to wear it. I don't wear mine anymore. I keep it on my nightstand."

He lifted the necklace. "I want to put it on." Tori had to help with the clasp since his arm was still in a sling.

"Mom and I spread his ashes at St. Peter's Catholic church, at the butterfly garden."

"Thank you." Tobias touched the vial. "This is all new to me. I'm not sure what to think."

"It will take time."

Tori placed a hand on his forearm. "Will you ever forgive me for not telling you?"

"Yeah, I already did."

Tobias stood and took the stack of pictures and one of the baby's hospital bracelets. "I better get going."

He studied her for a long time. "I'm sorry you had to go through it alone. If I'd known, I'm not sure I would have been able to be here. The military wouldn't have sent me back so soon after arriving, especially not during wartime. So I screwed up. I should've talked to you before joining."

"It's over now, Tobias. I'm just glad you know now. I imagine you will have to grieve since you just found out. So give yourself time and be patient. With your accident and all, you need to relax for a bit."

WITH A WEDDING coming up the next week, he wasn't

exactly giving himself much time. Tobias wondered if he should tell Tori, but then decided it wasn't her concern. Although they'd always be connected with the past, it was best to break all contact with her.

Her nose was pink from crying and he fought against it but, in the end, he gave up. He hugged Tori against him, a farewell to the one woman he'd never stop loving.

"Goodbye."

Her eyes searched his. "Yeah...bye."

CHAPTER FOURTEEN

Halfway to his ranch, Tobias pulled over and climbed out of his truck. He hobbled to the front of the vehicle and leaned on it, the entire time searching the sky. It wasn't as if some sort of angel would appear in the darkness and give him a message, but he needed something.

How could it be that he'd missed something so monumental? Although he'd told Tori all was forgiven, anger and resentment circled like buzzards over his head.

A part of him wanted to keep driving and get away from it all.

In the distance, headlights appeared. As they got closer, he realized it was a red Jeep and moving fast. He almost laughed. Not exactly an angel headed his way. Most people, upon first seeing his twin, would probably think him the opposite.

What the hell was Luke doing? The man was driving like a bat out of hell.

Tobias reached into his window and flashed the

lights. The Jeep skidded to a stop and his twin got out of the car and hurried to him.

"What happened?" The hollowness in his eyes made Tobias think twice and not utter a stupid comeback. It didn't take much for Luke to go into flashback mode some days.

"Heading home from visiting Tori. Learned some shitty news and needed an explanation."

Luke didn't say anything. Luke's gaze roamed over him as if to assess if he lied. "What news?"

This was the first time he'd talk about what happened, about Thomas. First, he ran a shaky hand through his hair.

"Found out Tori was pregnant when I went overseas. She lost the baby. A boy."

When his brother didn't speak, he continued. "Tori says I don't have to feel guilty. But damn, she had a nervous breakdown because I left and that may have caused her to lose the baby. It kinda makes it my fault."

"I would feel guilty if it was me. Why did she pick now to tell you? That was like over twenty years ago."

Tobias shrugged. "We were arguing as usual. I said something stupid and she let it slip. I don't think she ever planned to tell me."

Luke came and leaned against the front of the truck with his arms crossed over his chest. "Damn. I guess the truth always does come out."

"Yep."

"I suppose you and I aren't ever going to have kids,"

Luke said.

Tobias thought about it. "Mimi wants to have a couple. I'm not so sure. Hell, I'm almost forty-six."

"Me, too," Luke said with a chuckle.

"Where were you headed?" Tobias asked, wondering why Luke wasn't in a hurry to leave now.

"To find you. Tori called and said you might be upset."

They stood in silence for a long time. Luke allowed him time to think and get his shit together. Finally, Tobias convinced his twin he was okay and headed home to rest.

THE HOUSE WAS quiet when Tobias arrived. He figured Ernest and Henry had gone to bed. Both went to sleep early and got up unnaturally early as well.

The dogs roused at his arrival and he walked to the back deck with them. The animals took off into the darkness, probably searching for critters to chase and he lowered to a chair.

When his phone buzzed, he answered it.

"When are you getting here? I have to finish packing and make sure to have all my documents. Did you find your birth certificate?" Mimi started peppering him with questions and he waited for her to take a breath.

"We've gone over this several times. I've got everything I need. We don't fly out for two days. I'll throw stuff in the overnight bag and head there the day after tomorrow."

"Head where? To my place or to the airport."

Tobias rolled his eyes. "Mimi, we just talked about this specific topic earlier today. You said you would hire a car since you live out of the way."

"No, maybe you should pick me up. That way we arrive at the airport together."

"The Billings airport is not that big," Tobias replied, becoming annoyed.

He could hear rustling and then Mimi crunching in his ear. "I'm so hungry. I spent the entire day shopping." She sighed. "You know what, maybe I'll just hire a car."

Tobias' finger lingered over the button to end the call. "I'll see you the day after tomorrow."

"Wait," Mimi interrupted and he felt bad. If she was about to tell him she loved him, he wasn't sure he could respond in kind.

"Yeah?"

"Oh, shoot, gotta go. I have to answer this call I've been waiting for it. I'll see you. Don't forget your birth certificate." She giggled and ended the call.

He stared at the cell display. What the hell was wrong with her? The woman was half-crazy at times. If it weren't for the long day he'd had, Tobias would have laughed.

TWO DAYS LATER, morning came way too soon. Tobias trudged to the front room with his overnight bag. He looked in the direction of the kitchen to find Ernest drinking coffee. His cousin lifted his gaze to him. "Ready to go? We need to get going."

"That might be why I'm carrying a bag and headed to the door," Tobias snapped.

"No coffee? Oh, hell. We are not driving to the airport with you in a bitchy mood."

This was his life. Damned family. "Let's go, please."

Ernest's eyebrows lifted and then his gaze narrowed. "I'm only going to ask you this once. Are you sure, absolutely sure, about this?"

Tobias turned away and walked out the front door, the dogs trotting along. He looked down to the two trusting faces. "I'll see you two in a couple days. Be good." Both wagged their tails as if understanding. He knew they didn't, but it was nice to see them rush off barking, tongues hanging out upon spotting the horse trainer arriving.

The trip was about an hour and a half. He called Mimi several times, but she did not answer. Tobias figured she was headed to the airport and didn't hear the phone.

They arrived two hours before his flight since Ernest was always a stickler for being early to things. Once again, Tobias called Mimi.

"Why isn't she answering?" He looked around.

Ernest looked across the lobby. "Maybe she's going through security."

"Yeah. That's possible. Thanks for the ride." Tobias

held out his hand. "See you when I'm married."

His cousin took his hand. "I wish you the best. See you in a few days."

Since he didn't have to check a bag, Tobias went directly to security, but then decided not to go through just yet.

He waited for another half-hour and called. Still nothing from Mimi. Finally, an hour before the flight when they began to announce boarding, he couldn't wait any longer and he went through security.

His heart plummeted when he arrived at the gate. There were only about twenty people waiting to board. Mimi was not among them. He went to the gate.

The man behind the counter looked up. "How can I help you, sir?"

"Can you tell me if Emmaline Murphy has checked in for something? We're traveling together and she's not here."

He shook his head. "No one by that name has approached the counter and I can't give you any information about any ticket changes."

"Thanks." He turned away as the same guy announced the first zone for boarding.

Tobias was watching the plane taxiing away from the gate when his phone dinged. Tobias was too furious to read it. If Mimi was angry because they didn't swing by to pick her up, he was going to lose it.

"Where are you?" he said without preamble.

"I'm sorry," Mimi said, sounding more petulant than sorry. "Remember that call I got yesterday?"

How could the woman be so irritating? "What call?"

"The call last night when I hung up. It was my lawyer. My ex didn't sign the divorce papers right. Then I found out it would take a few weeks anyway. I thought once he signed the papers we would be divorced."

"You're married?" he hissed into the phone, already heading back toward the exit. "What the fuck?"

She huffed. "We met at a restaurant weeks ago and he signed the papers. Don't cuss at me. I told you when we met."

"You said you were recently single."

"Anyway," she continued ignoring his comment. "Want me to pick you up? We can set another date."

"There won't be another date." Tobias' hand was shaking so bad he had to tap on the display twice to finally end the call.

When he went down the escalator toward the exit, Ernest was standing by the baggage claim. He waved at Tobias.

"What are you doing here?"

"Your mom had asked Eric to do some checking on Mimi. He thought she might still be married, but we couldn't find out for sure. Mimi called me a few minutes ago to ask if she could still get married in Vegas if she was married in Montana. I figured she wasn't going to show up, so I turned around."

"Don't say another word." Tobias pointed at Ernest's face. "I mean it."

"Can I laugh?"

He fought not to crack a smile. "No."

CHAPTER FIFTEEN

"**A**RE YOU SURE you're okay?" Allison held her wine glass halfway to her lips. "You don't look good."

Just because she felt like bawling her eyes out and screaming didn't mean she wasn't fine. Anyone in her shoes would be hysterical. Tobias, the only man she'd ever truly loved now belonged to a blonde who had less sense than flattened road kill. Tori took a shaky breath.

"Stop staring at me. I'm just a bit overwhelmed at the idea of the whole wedding thing."

"You should have told him how you feel. Maybe he wouldn't have gotten married." Allison took a sip of wine and slid a look to the couch where Taylor was. He'd been watching a movie but, by his soft snores, he didn't find it to be interesting.

Tori leaned forward and refilled her glass. "I couldn't do that. We don't get along. Just because you love someone doesn't always mean you belong together. He made a choice to marry that woman, so he must be in love. He's moved on."

"True," Allison replied with a sigh. "But I think he's still in love with you."

"There are different types of love," Tori said and flipped her agenda open. "Let's set a schedule for the next two weeks. We have a few things to accomplish before the book event that you volunteered me and Leah for."

They talked for a few minutes and made plans. Allison called Leah and had her on speakerphone as they set a schedule for the event that was to take place at Tori's restaurant. The distraction was good. For those few moments, she didn't have to think about Tobias and what was happening in Las Vegas.

But her mind kept going back to what happened that day. Tobias was married now. It felt surreal.

Allison closed her agenda. "I feel good about our time table. I think the cake theme is so cool. I have a great recipe in mind for mine."

Ding. Ding. Tori pulled out her cell phone and looked at the message. It was from Alec, the veterinarian.

She texted back that she'd call him in a few moments.

Just then, Taylor's phone rang and he reached for it. "Yeah, what's up?"

He sat up and looked over toward them. "Give me a second. I have questions." He stood and stretched. Then with his phone to his ear, he went into the bedroom.

Allison watched him. "I wonder who's calling him. He always gets the best gossip but doesn't always share. I have to beg, borrow and steal to get him to tell me anything." Her friend's brow crinkled as she continued to look toward the bedroom.

"You are so nosy," Tori teased. "It's probably something only guys would find interesting."

"That's true," Allison said with a giggle. "If it's one of his cousins, they only ever talk about cows and dogs. Sometimes they plan a get-together to do something exciting like grill hotdogs." Allison's flat tone was comical. Obviously, her friend didn't consider the Hamiltons the most exciting family when planning gatherings.

An hour later, Tori walked into her place and lowered to the couch while calling Alec.

His voice was deep and soothing. Tori closed her eyes and envisioned his face. He was nice and definitely someone she could see dating long term.

"I want to see you again."

Tori nodded even though he couldn't see her. "I'd love to see you as well. What do you have in mind?"

"I can cook dinner if you wish?" There was hesitancy in his voice. "Or a movie would be cool, too."

Tori made a decision. If she was going to move on, it was best to do so full-heartedly. "You know what? Dinner at your place sounds perfect. What time?"

Her phone dinged. It was Allison. She didn't bother reading. This was the time to consider what to do and perhaps take some time for herself and make some decisions.

The book club was a good beginning. She'd also joined a local hiking group and was considering teaching cooking classes to local teens.

She went to the couch and began typing plans into her laptop. Things were going to change. Soon, she'd be too busy and satisfied with her own life to care what happened in other people's lives.

THE NEXT DAY went by fast. It was their busiest in a long time. People who were traveling through to go to the next town over for a conference stopped in Laurel Creek for lunch and dinner. The restaurant barely had a table empty as they seated more people. Whenever there was a short lull, Tori and Jessie took advantage and helped prep in the kitchen.

Just before the dinner rush, Tori stepped outside for a short break. She noticed Allison was also doing brisk business. Her flower shop always attracted the attention of visitors to Laurel Creek. Planters overflowing with bright flowers and hanging baskets with long, bright green vines spilling over their sides made an inviting entrance to the shop.

Down the street, the café's door was open as a group of people entered. Just then, two couples came to the restaurant and Tori followed them in. Three more hours and she'd be free to head home.

By the time she arrived at Alec's apartment, Tori was tired but energized at the same time. Wearing a simple green shift dress and off-white cardigan, along with beige flat sandals, she felt pretty and ready to spend time with a good-looking man.

Alec opened the door. Dressed in jeans and a navy polo shirt, he looked handsome and casual.

His gaze roamed over her and his lips curved. "You're always a lovely sight."

"Thank you." Tori held up a bag with two bottles of wine. "I wasn't sure what you were cooking, so I brought white and a red. Pinot Grigio and Cabernet."

"I'm grilling. How about steaks and asparagus."

He took the wine from her and leaned forward to place a soft kiss on her lips.

Deciding not to decipher how she felt about the kiss, Tori followed him into the kitchen. When he put the bag down, she moved closer and then wrapped her arms around his neck. "What time is dinner?"

The corners of his lips moved. "How about I let you decide?"

They weren't talking about dinner. She wanted to get any physical intimacy between them over. The awkward first time would be enjoyable, of that she was sure, but afterward, they could move on and learn more about each other.

Alec responded with enthusiasm when she pulled him down for a deep kiss that soon became heated. His hands traveled down her back to cup her butt.

IT WAS MIDNIGHT by the time Tori parked at her house. She pulled into her driveway and almost made it to her door when her neighbors called out.

"Hey there, Tori. Are you okay? It's very late."

She took a deep breath. The older neighbor meant well, but he was terribly nosy.

"I'm fine, Mr. Walter. Just went out with friends."

"That's what I told that Hamilton fella. He sat out here in his truck for an hour waiting on ya."

Her heart thudded until it echoed in her ears. "Who?"

"One of the twins. The one that just had that car wreck." The old man was animated now that he had her attention. "I know it was him since he's got a leg brace. Otherwise, you can't tell them apart. They sure are identical."

Tori let out a long, shaky breath. This could not be happening. "What was he doing here? He say anything?"

"We talked for about a minute." Mr. Walter gave her a cheeky smile. "He said he's been doing physical therapy twice a week and still limps."

It was best to back away from Mr. Walter. He would continue to talk for hours if given the chance. Tori took a step back. "I'll give him a call. Thank you, Mr. Walter."

"He and his brother, they're both war heroes ya know?"

"Good night, Mr. Walter."

"Went to war myself. I was much younger…"

Tori escaped into her dark house and leaned against the door.

She raced to her bedroom and fell face first onto the bed. Tori fought to keep from reaching for her cell. Whatever was Tobias doing back in town? And more importantly, why had he been waiting for her? It made no sense whatsoever.

The moon was full. Its light shined through the thin curtains on her bedroom window casting beautiful shadows across her bed.

As much as she wanted to revel in the wonderful night she'd had with Alec, a part of her was angry. Why couldn't she have a bit of peace? If anything, after all this time, she'd finally moved on and enjoyed a wonderful night of lovemaking and a good meal.

That damned Tobias, he ruined everything. Her heart was shattered and he refused to allow it to heal and move on.

Tori punched the pillow, rolling to her side in an attempt to get comfortable. Finally, as slumber edged in, her cell phone dinged.

It was a text from Allison.

Call me in the morning. I have some good juicy gossip.

Tori blew out a breath. The nosy part of her really wanted to call and find out what happened. But for a few hours, she preferred to bask in the afterglow of finally having sex. The first time in years that she'd had sex with someone other than Tobias.

Then she noticed a big bright number one next to the message icon. A part of her knew it was a mistake to listen to it, but her fingers moved independently.

"Tori. It's Tobias. We should talk."

By the hollowness in his voice, she wondered if he was still having a hard time processing their son's death. Perhaps he'd returned from the wedding sooner because he had questions and wanted to probe deeper, ask more questions and such.

Tomorrow would be soon enough to find out. Did everyone have so much drama after a date with a new guy?

Tori didn't allow the continuing thoughts to linger. Instead, she allowed sleep to take over.

CHAPTER SIXTEEN

I T WAS OBVIOUS by ten in the morning it was going to be another busy day and Mindy didn't mind it one bit. Already, she'd run out of muffins and there were second and third batches of them in the oven. The air smelled wonderful, the aroma of the baking wafting out the door bringing even more customers inside.

When the bell over the door dinged, she didn't bother looking up. Her lips curved at hearing a woman telling her friend how hard it was to pick a favorite.

"Good morning, ladies," Mindy said, smiling. Upon noting they both studied the baked items, she added, "How about I start you with a beverage while you decide what you want?"

It was then she caught sight of Eric. In full uniform, he stood just inside the door. A younger woman was asking him directions, her eyes wandering over him when he pointed out directions on a map she'd produced.

The woman didn't need directions. Any moment now, she'd give him her number or come up with some sort of ploy to get more of his time. Seeming to sense her regard, he looked toward the counter and winked. The man knew what the woman was doing.

Upon noticing what he did, the young woman said something and he replied. Unfortunately, Mindy couldn't attempt at lip reading because the two women had finally decided to buy one of each muffin. She packaged up the golden raisin, triple chocolate, banana nut and blueberry muffins in a pastry box.

The women scurried to a table with their muffins and Mindy's employee followed them with their lattes.

She had a hard time taking orders with Eric there. After not coming in to the coffee shop for days, he'd made an appearance only after they'd made love. If he was going to let her know he was leaving, she wasn't sure it would be possible to keep from crying. It was best to stop him before he did.

"Hey, beautiful," he greeted her while placing his travel mug on the counter. "I was hoping to grab you for a few minutes, but it looks as if you're slammed today."

Heat surfaced on her cheeks. "Yes, it's been busy since yesterday. It will probably continue through the weekend." Mindy turned around to pour his coffee.

"Can I take you out for dinner then?"

At least he was being decent enough to tell her in person. Mindy released a shaky breath. "Dinner sounds great. Where?"

He shrugged. "How about if I pick you up at six? We can decide then."

There were only two restaurants in Laurel Creek, three if you counted Shooters. Which she didn't.

She was pretty sure Victoria's was out of the question. It would be hard enough to be told a relationship is over without it being around people she was good friends with. Mindy realized he waited for a response.

"We can choose then," she replied with a smile. "See you at six.

Once he walked out, the young woman who'd been flirting with him walked up and looked up at the menu. "I'll take a banana nut and a tall coffee, black, no sugar or creamer," she rattled off. "The policeman said he was your boyfriend."

Mindy was caught off guard. "Umm-yes."

The woman looked down her nose at Mindy and seemed to find her lacking. "Impressive."

What the hell did that mean? Mindy frowned at the woman. "What is it you find impressive?"

Mindy's helper slid her a glance and rang up the woman's order while Mindy narrowed her eyes at the woman.

The annoying woman gave her a one-shoulder shrug. "Just that he's very attractive and you…well you didn't seem overly friendly to him. If he were my…"

"But he isn't," Mindy interrupted and turned away to an older couple. Thank God for them. Otherwise, she would have said something horrible. Mindy decided they'd get a free pastry for their presence alone.

AT SIX O'CLOCK that night, Eric was at Mindy's door. She'd decided they'd not have dinner out. If the man was going to break up with her, it was best not to have it done in a public place.

"Please, come in," she said as she stepped back to allow him room. Eric gave her a puzzling look for a moment then walked inside.

When she motioned for him to sit, he removed his jacket. "Is something wrong?"

Mindy almost laughed out loud. "If you don't mind, I'd rather we talk here before going anywhere. You didn't make reservations did you?"

He shook his head. "Nope. Just planned to go to Victoria's."

Just as she thought. A public dumping. "Would you like a glass of wine?"

Once again he studied her. "Okay." He said the word slowly almost as a question and Mindy walked off before he did ask one.

"Won't be but a minute."

When Mindy returned to the living room, her stomach was in knots, her knees barely kept her upright. That she was fighting back tears before the man even started his "since I'm moving, we should just end it" speech, Mindy waterworks were a huge possibility.

"Are you sure you're all right?" Eric stood and took the wine glasses from her, placed them on the coffee table and pulled her against him for a hug.

Whatever expensive cologne he wore made her take a

deep breath. She loved the way he smelled. Eric's finger combed through her hair and he cupped her chin and kissed her. The warmth of his lips soothed every part of her. When he suckled at her bottom lip, a soft moan escaped and Mindy relaxed against him.

"I can never get enough of you," Eric mumbled against her mouth. "You're the reason I can't leave."

Mindy pushed back, suddenly aware of what he'd just said. "What do you mean?"

"I turned the job down. I have too much going on here. If Tobias moves to Billings, my uncle asked if I want to take over at the ranch."

So he wasn't going to repeat what he'd said at first. "What about what you want? What makes you happy?" Mindy's brain was screaming for her to shut up. Less than five minutes earlier, she was about to dissolve into hysterics over him leaving and now, for some stupid reason, she wanted to argue that he'd chosen to stay.

"Mindy." Eric kissed her again. It was hard to kiss him and not wish for it to linger. "Look at me," he persisted. "What's wrong with you? You don't want me to stay?"

Tugging at his hands, she bit her bottom lip before speaking. "Sit down, let's toast."

Her eyes locked on his, she held up her glass. "I celebrate your decision. The reason I've been a bit off today is that I was expecting you to dump me, to end things."

The corners of his lips curved up. "If anything, I was trying to figure out how to convince you to come with me. With our relationship being so new, I figured you'd turn me down."

"Seriously?" Mindy blinked back tears. "I would have said yes. I am in love with you, Eric."

He looked down and Mindy wanted to kick herself. Had she really just blurted out that she loved him? Now he was probably figuring out how to respond and not hurt her feelings.

Eric blew out a breath and stood up. Mindy wasn't sure what to do, so she stood, too. "You don't have to leave. I understand if you feel differently. I mean we've just started dating. Only slept together once…"

"Shut up," Eric said, bringing his mouth over hers. Pulling her against him, she was instantly aware that he was fully aroused as his erection pressed into her stomach. Mindy wrapped her arms around his waist and pulled him tighter against her.

Eric pulled back and lifted her chin so he could look into her eyes. Then taking a step back, he reached for his jacket.

Mindy wasn't sure whether to stare at his face or the huge bulge in his pants. Why was he getting his jacket? Did he just tell her to shut up? This was the most confusing evening.

"Every relationship moves at a different pace. I've been in love with you for years, Mindy. I was a coward who didn't trust myself to say the right thing. I hate how long I prolonged finally asking you out." He took out a small velvet box from his jacket. "Marry me."

If her eyes could've fallen out of their sockets they would have. But thankfully, they were tethered.

"Yes!" Mindy threw herself against him with so much force they tumbled onto the couch.

Within minutes, there was a trail of clothing from the living room to her bedroom and Mindy could not contain what she felt. So much so that she began to cry, making Eric immediately pull away and look down at her.

"Did I hurt you?"

She shook her head, embarrassed by the outburst of emotion. "No. I'm happy."

His lips quivered at the corners just a bit. "You'll have to tell me what to do in instances like this."

"Kiss me."

His mouth was instantly over hers, the taste of him mingling with the saltiness of her tears. He felt so very good, the weight of him atop her, the anchor she'd been missing for so long.

"I want to make love until morning," he mumbled in her ear. Mindy sighed, sliding her hands down his back to cup his firm butt.

"My sentiments exactly."

She'd never tire of his kisses, his touch and the wonderful way they fit together.

"You feel so perfect," she whispered as he thrust into her.

CHAPTER SEVENTEEN

WHEN LUKE GALLOPED toward him, Tobias immediately concentrated on his brother. The lingering sadness that had enveloped him was instantly replaced with concern for Luke.

The tension in Tobias' shoulders went away at Luke's relaxed expression. It was gratifying to see the way marriage to Leah had changed Luke, the calming effect that allowed his brother to keep the storms in his mind at bay.

Tobias wasn't fool enough to think Luke was miraculously cured. Luke would always have PTSD, but that it was managed to a point where there was normality in his life was good enough.

"Heard what happened," Luke said as he studied his brother for a beat. In those few seconds, it was as if his twin read every thought and shared his emotions. Sometimes, it sucked being a twin.

"Yep, suppose I dodged that bullet," Tobias replied with a hollow chuckle.

Luke didn't even crack a smile. "You okay?"

Why did he have to ask that? Tobias urged his horse to move. "Yeah. You?"

"Leah's gone for a couple days to help her dad with some company stuff. So I'm hanging with the dogs. Eating pizza and drinking beer for dinner."

Being that Luke loved to cook and was the main one to do so, Tobias figured it was a break from it for his brother.

"So much for scoring a dinner invite," Tobias muttered. "I can have shitty pizza and beer at home."

"Who says my pizza is shitty?"

At the realization Luke made it from scratch, Tobias' ears perked. "You making some tonight?"

"I might."

A wave of what felt like cement hit Tobias. He could barely breathe. Not sure how, he managed to dismount and stalk in a circle, his lungs screaming for air.

"What the fuck?" he gasped out. "Shit. I. Can't. Br…"

Luke came up beside him, not freaking out, but quite the opposite. He put a hand on Tobias' shoulder. "Look at me. Now huff out air a couple times."

At first, it was ridiculous to huff when he couldn't get any oxygen in, but he tried and after a couple times, he gulped in air. His brother guided him to bend over and put his hands on his knees.

"What the hell?" Tobias said. "Am I having a heart attack?"

"Nah. Panic attack. Anxiety."

"Shit. Right. Nope, I think I better go to the doctor. I'm not in a good place mentally, but that doesn't mean I want to die."

Gingerly, Tobias straightened and took a deep breath. His chest didn't feel tight. It had been his lungs that had been burning.

He glared at Luke. "Why would I be panicking? Or freaking out?"

"You tell me." His brother was ever so eloquent. Then again, Luke didn't have to say much to get a point across.

Tobias stared at his twin for a long time. "I have...had a son."

Luke didn't react. Instead, he watched him, guarding him, protecting him.

Although Luke already knew the details, Tobias repeated them. "Tori was pregnant and he died, right after being born. A boy." The words came out stilted, as if told by someone who didn't quite understand the subject. "She didn't tell me. I fucking hate her for that. If I would have stayed, maybe he wouldn't have died. Shit. I don't know."

He didn't realize he was crying until a tear rolled into his mouth, the salty taste taking Tobias by surprise.

"I can't ever forgive her for that, Luke. Do you have any idea? Shit I don't know what to feel. What to think."

"Why didn't she tell you?"

Tobias looked up at the sky. "I guess because she

didn't want me to stay just because she was pregnant. Man, I know she was a kid. But that kind of shit, you don't keep to yourself and then dump it on someone twenty years later."

When Luke came closer and pressed his forehead to his brother's, Tobias realized he was sobbing uncontrollably. He was grieving for the little boy, his son.

"I don't know what to fucking feel." He allowed his head to fall onto Luke's shoulder and his brother remained still as a statue. "What am I supposed to feel?"

"Pained. Angry. Betrayed." Luke summed up exactly what he felt.

Tobias jerked away and swiped away the tears with the back of his hand.

"Did you know?" Tobias directed his anger toward Luke. "Did Mom tell you? She knew. I'm pissed at her, too."

"Nah, I didn't. Mom probably felt it wasn't her place to tell you. This was something Tori had to do. Explain it. Did she?"

Tobias nodded. "She feels guilty about it. Shit, I guess it wasn't her fault. I suppose not really mine either."

They walked for a few minutes. The time allowed Tobias to get his shit together. Admittedly, he felt a bit embarrassed about crying. However, if he were to be honest, he and Luke had always been open with emotions.

"It's not too late, you know?" Luke said, his gaze

forward. "You and Tori. She's young enough."

Tobias stopped abruptly and gave his brother an incredulous look. "What are you talking about? She and I are barely on speaking terms."

"That doesn't mean you're not in love."

"Since when are you a romantic?" Tobias attempted at humor, but it came out dry.

As was the norm for his brother, Luke only stared back at him. A look that said, "I know you more than you know yourself."

A COUPLE HOURS later, the twins walked into Shooters for what could be a late lunch or early dinner. A pretty brunette who worked there did a double take reminding Tobias of how often it used to happen when they were younger and hung out all the time. Lately, they rarely did and because of that, sometimes Tobias forgot that he and Luke were identical.

"I know you're probably used to this…" the young woman's gaze moved down his body and up Luke's. "…but you're like every woman's dream."

Tobias looked to Luke. "I've never heard that, have you?"

The more menacing of the two, Luke narrowed his eyes and took a step closer to the young woman, who seemed to be rethinking the flirtation. "You volunteering?" Only Tobias knew Luke was kidding.

"Oh. No. I was just…" She took a step backward

and giggled nervously.

Ernest materialized with a beer in his right hand. He ignored Luke and looked at the woman. "Don't pay any attention to him. He likes to intimidate people for no reason."

The woman gave them a quick smile and hurried away.

Tobias moved to stand just a bit closer to Ernest than Luke. "Don't start shit, Cuz. Don't need to get kicked out of here again."

Ernest slid a quick look to Luke. "Henry and I have a table over here. If you want to hang out with us."

They went to where Ernest's partner was. A different server, a slender guy this time, placed a pitcher of beer on the table and two glasses. "Would you like something to eat?"

They ordered a shitload of wings and another pitcher. It had been a while since Tobias had spent time out with family. The whole Mimi thing had him staying away from them in an effort to not hear any crap about her. Damn, he supposed they'd been right. Of course, he'd never admit it out loud.

Henry was easy-going and patient, the perfect partner for Ernest who was almost as much of a hot head as Luke. Luke eyed Ernest and huffed. "I'd think you'd be too much of a snob to hang out here."

"Obviously, you shouldn't be allowed to think," Ernest replied, taking a long swig of beer.

As usual, Henry defused the situation by piling fries

on a plate and sliding it in front of Luke. "I hear you and Leah are selling the cattle. What brought this on?"

They began to discuss the fact Luke and Leah were going to open a horse ranch for service members with PTSD. The idea had merit and Tobias was proud of what his brother planned to do.

"Have you heard from Mimi?" Ernest asked Tobias.

"No and I don't expect to," Tobias replied. "I ended it with her."

Henry grinned. "I'm going to miss that woman. She made me laugh. What a ditz."

Tobias nodded. "Yeah, she is one of a kind, that's for sure."

Just then, Ernest looked over Tobias' shoulder. "Taylor's here. Texted earlier, says he's got some interesting news."

CHAPTER EIGHTEEN

O NE PUPPY WHIMPERED when Tori picked up its sibling. She put the puppy down and both made the high-pitched, unhappy noise.

"They're used to always being together," the woman who fostered them said. She then picked them both up and handed them to Tori.

The little dogs were fat, fluffy and they smelled of innocence and sleepless nights. They were perfect and adorable. Since they'd been abandoned, the foster mother had no idea what breed they were or how big they'd get. Judging by the petite paws, Tori guessed they'd not be very big.

"I can't possibly take both. I am hardly ever home and my cottage is tiny." She kissed both fluffy faces and placed them down. Oblivious, the puppies began to play, chasing each other and pouncing.

The woman nodded. "I understand. After a few days, I'm sure they'd be fine if separated." She didn't sound convinced. Both she and the woman watched as the two bundles of fur continued to play.

"What will happen to them if both are not adopted?"

The woman smiled. "I run a no-kill rescue. The dogs remain here permanently if they are not adopted. My husband gripes about it all the time. Currently, we have six grown dogs and these two troublemakers."

They were across the street from the café at the town square. The woman and her husband had agreed to bring the puppies to play in the park that afternoon so Tori could see them. She'd fallen in love when seeing them online and they were even more adorable in person.

"I don't know what to do. I want a dog but, at the same time, it may not be the right time." For some reason, she sniffed. The last thing she needed to do was to cry about puppies.

"How hard can it be? Either you take them or you don't." Tobias' deep voice made Tori and the woman turn to look.

Upon hearing the timbre of his voice, the puppies raced toward him. It was then she noticed Luke was just a bit further back. The puppy foster mom smiled at Luke. "How are the dogs doing? Rosie is one of them, right?"

Luke nodded. "Both are doing great."

The last thing she needed was to run into Tobias. Instantly, the fact she'd been intimate with another man came to the front of her mind.

"I better go. I'll think about it and call later," Tori told the woman and then turned on her heel, determined to get away from Tobias.

Luke touched her arm as she passed him. "You two should talk."

"We did," Tori replied. "There isn't much more to say."

It struck her how different Luke was now than before going to war. His eyes seemed to soften. "There is a lot more." With those cryptic words, he walked over to play with the delighted puppies.

"I came by last night," Tobias said, catching up with her. "You were out, or not answering the door."

It was best to not reply. The last thing she needed to do was discuss her love life with Tobias. "I heard."

"Didn't get married after all."

When her stomach lurched and her chest tightened, Tori wasn't sure what to make of the strange sensations. To make matters worse, she had to take a deep breath before speaking.

"I'm sorry."

He shrugged, his hazel eyes boring into her. "I was forcing the issue. It worked out for the best."

"So she broke things off?" Tori had a hard time picturing that. If anything, Mimi seemed determined to get Tobias to marry her no matter what.

Tobias shrugged. "A legal thing. But, yeah, I guess you can say that."

Without thinking, Tori slugged him in the arm. "Don't you find it crazy that fate has to step in, otherwise you'd marry someone you obviously are not in love with?"

"Can I see you later? I need to talk to you. About…"

Tori cut him off by putting her hand up, palm facing him. "I really don't think we have anything at all to discuss anymore, Tobias. The past is gone, we should move on."

"I'm having a hard time." He swallowed, all the while his gaze pinning hers, keeping Tori from moving. If he only knew how much power he had over every one of her senses.

He let out breath. "Just need to ask you some questions. Can I walk you home?"

In actuality, she'd planned to remain at the park and spend time with a puppy, but now she had no dog. She didn't want to adopt two and she wasn't sure anymore if she really wanted the responsibility of a dog, much less a puppy.

"Fine. But I don't know what more can possibly be said."

He remained silent. Taking her elbow, he guided her to the sidewalk. They walked slowly, each in their own thoughts for a few minutes. From the corner of her eye, she admired his profile. He was still the most handsome man she'd ever met. His brown hair glistened in the sunlight. There were a few gray hairs sprinkled at his temple, which only made him more attractive. Tobias was tall, six foot five, muscular with wide shoulders and a flat stomach. From what she knew, he worked out regularly and by the fact he'd raced and helped the team win the relay, Tori guessed he ran, also.

It was not fair that he had such a pull on her. If anything, she needed to feel dislike of him. But they had history, and ties that would bind them forever.

"Why are you looking at me like you want to strangle my neck?" He lifted a brow and looked to her. When his eyes traveled to her lips, Tori frowned and bit her bottom lip.

"I was considering our history and the fact I don't really hate you."

His lips twitched. "I don't really hate you either."

When his eyes narrowed in thought, Tori frowned. "What?"

"Come with me. Let's go for a drive."

"A drive. I really don't think that's a good idea. What exactly do you want to talk about? She stopped walking and put her hands on both hips. "You're acting strange. Well, stranger than usual."

"And you always make things difficult. I want to talk. I need to ask you some questions. And I think if we drive somewhere besides your house or my place, then the neutral setting will be perfect."

Her stomach tightened. Whatever he was going to say must be really bad that he wanted her not to have a way to escape from it. Tori wasn't about to show any weakness or let him know that being alone with him terrified her. She was dating Alec now and it was time to let him know.

"Fine. But not too far that I can't get away from you

if you piss me off."

"If anything, you'll be the one to make me want to run. You have such a way with things."

"What is that supposed to mean?"

He looked away from her with an expression of innocence. "Nothing. Come on, my truck is over here." He took her elbow and shouted goodbye to Luke who waved them off.

THOUGHTS OF HOW to tell Tori the truth tumbled around in his head. Tobias thought of one way to explain what he had to say and then changed his mind. How hard could it be to be totally honest, to tell her exactly how he felt and what he hoped for?

Truth be told, he wasn't exactly sure what it was that would be the best for them. In a way, he agreed with Luke that, perhaps, it wasn't too late. There was a strong possibility that Tori could still have children and would agree to it. However, the odds were definitely not in his favor.

The attraction between them was tangible, so strong he instinctively knew when she entered a room or looked in his direction. The pull between them hadn't faded over the years. That they'd entered into a routine of insults and barbs had been a form of barrier. For him at least.

Tori seemed to take great delight in hurling put downs and insults at him. She'd actually become quite proficient, if he were to be honest.

"What are you chuckling about?" Tori asked, making him realized he'd been thinking out loud.

"About how good we are at trading insults. Over the years, I have to admit, I've looked forward to sparring with you."

She huffed. "I will say you're particularly good at it. I have to work to be mean. It seems to come naturally to you."

"I'm not a cruel person," he scoffed. "Everyone says I'm a nice guy. Mrs. Barbara, whom I help out, says I'm a sweetie."

"You've got her snowed."

Enjoying the familiarity of the conversation, Tobias lifted a brow. "Allison and Leah both often invite me to dinner. They like having me around."

"Both of them like feeding strays," Tori quipped. "They don't keep any of them though."

Tobias chuckled. "You turned down a pair of puppies who were crying because they wanted to be together. That," he said the last work with a sharp emphasis, "is very mean. Villain mean."

"It is, isn't it? I keep thinking about the poor little things. They are so cute." She sniffed.

Tobias immediately regretted bringing up the subject of the puppies. He had no idea she'd been fretting about it. "Bringing two dogs into a home is a lot of work, two puppies even more. With your long hours, it would have been hard for them. You'd have to leave them home alone for long hours."

"It wouldn't have been fair to them, right?" There was hope in her voice and Tobias wanted to hug and reassure her.

"No, it wouldn't have been fair. I was just picking on you. So see, I'm bad at being mean."

Tori gave him a playful punch in the shoulder. "So where exactly are you taking me?" She peered out the window. "Please tell me we're not going to the Lookout."

That was exactly where he'd been headed. They'd gotten engaged there, it was at the Lookout that they'd shared their first kiss and where they'd made love for the first time. He couldn't help but smile at the memory of the clumsy, awkward moment. It had been Tori's first time and she'd cried when he'd taken her virginity. He'd held her for a long time, anxious for her to calm down so he could show her how pleasant it could be.

"I haven't been up here in years, thought it would be cool to walk around up there." He lied. Just the week before, he'd brought the dogs for a walk there. But it was better than telling her he'd brought her there so it wouldn't be easy for her to run away when he spilled his guts.

The truck rocked side-to-side over the uneven terrain up the side of the mountain. Tori lowered the window and leaned back allowing the breeze to blow on her face. It was hard to tell if she was angry or pleased. Tobias leaned more toward annoyed by the slight crease between her brows.

"Want to listen to some music?"

"This is not a date," Tori said in a flat tone.

"Like I would date you."

"You would if I let you. But I wouldn't date you."

"You can barely resist me. My charms are like candy."

Tori opened her eyes so she could roll then. "Sour candy maybe."

Tobias chuckled and maneuvered the truck so that when he parked, they'd be facing the overlook.

When he cut off the engine, Tori climbed out and rounded the truck to where she could see the scenery below. From where she stood, the hill rolled softly down and onto another landing where one could picnic.

"This place is my life," she said in a soft voice. "Laurel Creek calls to me. I can't believe it's been so long since I've been up here."

Tobias came to stand next to her. "Hey, I can see the guys herding cattle at my place." He pointed in the direction of Hamilton lands. "Pretty cool."

"If you bring binoculars, you can spy on people from here. We used to do that when I was in middle school."

He chuckled. "You've always been a peeper."

Tori didn't deny it. "Why are we here?" She looked up at him, her dark gaze taking him in. "The truth, please."

This was it, do or die. He took a breath. "I brought you here because I want to tell you the truth. It's time to man up and be honest."

Her eyes widened. "I know you hate me for keeping the secret about Thomas. I know it will take time to forgive me."

Tobias wasn't about to be deterred. "I love you."

"You what?" Her eyes were as wide as saucers.

"It's always been you. You ruined me for other women. I have tried over these last twenty years to fall in love, but can't. That's why my marriage ended, I could not love her enough and she hated me for it." He raked a hand through his hair. "Shit, Tori, my heart is and will always be yours."

The wind blew her short hair back and forth as she stood as still as a statue and he itched to reach for her. Her eyes became shiny and he wondered if she were about to lose it.

She probably wouldn't cry, but she would scream at him and say she felt the opposite. Would never love him, and that there was no chance in hell they would ever be together.

Instead, she reached out with one hand and cupped his jaw. "Oh, Tobias." Blinking away tears, she swallowed visibly. "I don't know what to think right now."

"I'm not expecting a reply from you. Not right now anyway. I know this is coming out of left field. But I want to be honest with myself and with you. I'm tired of denying it, not just from you, but from myself." He placed his hand over the one at his jaw. "If there is any chance of us trying to work it out again, I want to take it. Think it over, okay?"

She let out a shaky breath. "Oh my God. You're serious."

"I am very serious. If it's possible, I love you more now than when I left for Afghanistan."

At the mention of the past, she looked away. "This is crazy. I really thought you wanted to talk about our son. I figured we'd end up arguing. You know, familiar territory."

She collapsed against him and he wrapped his arms around her.

It felt like he was home.

CHAPTER NINETEEN

TOBIAS DISMOUNTED AND removed the saddle from his horse.

"Hey, Boss," Jonathan, one of the new ranch hands, came to take the reins. "You've got company." He motioned toward the house and Tobias turned.

Sure enough, there was a familiar SUV parked in front of the house and Taylor's truck was also there. "Is something wrong?"

Jonathan shook his head. "I don't think so. Your mother is cooking."

"Why didn't you come get me?" Tobias yanked his leather gloves off.

"They said not to." Jonathan walked away whistling. The young man was about as carefree as a bird. Never seemed to get upset or particularly worried. Tobias shook his head.

After releasing the horse into the corral, he ambled to the house. Tobias took his time not sure what to expect.

"Hey, Son," his father called out from a rocker on

the porch. The labs were already at his dad's feet, looking up at the senior Hamilton as if he were a god.

Tobias neared and leaned forward to hug his father. "Didn't know you two planned to come to town."

"Talk to your mother, she's been anxious to come and spend time with you, Luke and Taylor. Something about a dream."

He walked inside and followed the smell of chicken roasting and conversation. Taylor and Luke were seated at the table with a slice of cake in front of them while his mother bustled around the kitchen.

Immediately, his chest constricted at the scene. He missed those days when he and the other two would sit while she fussed over them. He'd been a stupid teenager not to have cherished those moments.

"Hey, Mom," he greeted, going to her so they could embrace. She kissed his cheek and he returned the gesture. "Why do they have cake?"

"Don't hate," Luke said, lifting a huge chunk and popping it into his mouth.

"Sit down, I'll cut you a slice. I made this yesterday, made two actually since your sister was over with the kids."

He'd not seen Clara since the hospital. "We need to have a family gathering."

His mother smiled. "We have a wedding coming up. Eric and Mindy just got engaged."

Luke frowned. "I hate weddings."

"I still can't believe you and Leah snuck off and got

married at the courthouse. Cheated me out of wedding planning." By the soft smile directed at Luke, their mother didn't look particularly upset. "However, I can't picture you as a groom either. Probably scare half the guests away."

Everyone laughed.

Taylor looked toward the cake on the counter; he'd finished his slice. "Can I have more?"

His cousin seemed relaxed, even after receiving the news that his mother had died in prison. The strange thing was, it was as if he were relieved. It made sense. Her death closed that chapter of his life.

Tobias studied Taylor. "You should have a wedding. You deserve a wedding."

"I don't want a wedding, they're like a circus." Taylor had lived with them since middle school after his mother murdered his father and was incarcerated. Although cousins, Taylor was more like a brother to him and Luke.

"I'll speak to Allison," their mother quipped, cutting a slice and sliding it onto Taylor's plate. "Men don't understand these things."

She leaned on the counter. "I had a dream. Which one of you is giving me a grandchild?"

They all looked at each other.

"Leah can't have kids," Luke volunteered. "We don't want any."

Taylor shrugged. "We're not."

Everyone turned to Tobias.

"What? I don't even have a girlfriend right now."

Escape was the only answer. He took his cake plate and hurried out to the porch.

His father was still in the rocker. He looked up at Tobias and motioned to the other chair. "So, you're not getting married."

"Nope."

"Can't say I'm too sorry," his father admitted. "Though it would have been good to have a chance at a grandson to carry on the family name."

What was it with his parents suddenly caring about grandchildren? "Dad, Clara has a bunch of kids."

"None of them have the last name."

"We can talk one of her brood into it when they get older." Tobias laughed. "Hell, she and Tom probably won't notice."

His father chuckled. "That's true."

"Here comes trouble," Tobias said with a chuckle. Sure enough, a car pulled up and both Leah and Allison climbed out.

Leah approached first. "Mama Hamilton called." She lifted a bag of groceries from the back seat.

"We're here to cook, eat and drink," Allison added, lifting two wine bottles. They continued up the stairs and Tobias held the door for them to go inside.

"Nice to have family around, isn't it?" his father asked.

"It is." Tobias looked toward town. It would've been nicer if Tori were there. A truck appeared in the distance and just behind it another.

"Eric and Ernest are coming," he mumbled. "I better get Luke ready so he and Ernest don't bash each other's heads into a wall."

His father shook his head. "They'll behave around your mother."

IT WAS LIKE Thanksgiving. Tobias' plate was piled high with delicious food. Taylor and Eric talked shop, Luke and Ernest exchanged barbs and, all the while, Henry played referee. The women chatted about wedding stuff. Allison seemed to be warming to the idea of a wedding.

Thankfully, the discussion kept his mother too busy to question him about relationships.

Tori had promised to meet him again later that week and he wondered what would happen. If he were to be honest, he knew her reply would be that they be friends and move on. That it was too late for any kind of romantic involvement between them.

It would hurt but, eventually, hopefully, over time, the idea of them reuniting would fade.

And he was a three-ton gorilla.

If twenty years hadn't faded how he felt, then another twenty wouldn't help much either. He'd be single for the rest of his life and if Tori wasn't in the picture then he'd just have to accept it.

"Hello?" Allison waved a hand in front of his face. "Where are you at?"

He shrugged. "Just enjoying the company. That's all."

"I invited her, but she didn't feel comfortable because it's a family gathering." Allison lifted her wine glass. "I wish you two would work it out and admit how you feel."

"Ball's in her court," he replied in a low voice.

Allison gasped and everyone turned to her. She waved them away.

"It will be funny if all of you show up at the courthouse when Taylor and I get married next month."

"I plan to be there," his mother immediately said. "My Taylor is not getting married without cake."

"You can have a small reception," Mindy added.

Leah held up a hand. "Why don't you two exchange vows at Luke's and my place? We can have the judge come out and it will be simple. Family only."

Taylor's eyes rounded and met Allison's. "That sounds like a wedding."

"I think I can work with that. It sounds lovely, Leah, thank you," Allison said and the women began a new lively chatter.

Luke met his gaze from across the table, the solemn message loud and clear. His brother would always be there for him.

And that would have to be enough for Tobias if Tori didn't want to be part of his life.

CHAPTER TWENTY

"WE'RE HAVING A wedding." Taylor rolled to his side and gave Allison a look that she knew meant he wasn't sure he liked the idea.

She kissed him on the lips and smiled. "Looks like it. It will be simple, just us and the judge."

"And the entire Hamilton clan."

"You didn't really think your aunt would let you just get married at the courthouse, now did you?"

Allison loved his pensive look. He was such an amazing partner in life already. In actuality, she didn't need to be married to know Taylor would be beside her forever, but he was of the belief a couple should be married. Who was she to argue with a hunky man like him?

"You won't have to do a thing but show up," Allison murmured between kisses to his lips and jaw and then trailing her tongue down his neck.

"It will be casual. You can wear jeans and a green shirt."

"Green?"

"Yep, our wedding theme is green."

"Theme?" He cleared his throat, but then made a happy grunting sound when her hand traveled past his flat stomach.

"Oh, and we'll have cake, too."

There was a sharp inhale of breath when she finally took him in hand.

"Cake?" His voice deepened.

"Lots and lots of cake," Allison purred as she slipped under the covers.

"I like wedding planning." Taylor threaded his fingers through her curls.

LUKE OPENED THE back door to let their two dogs out. He watched as they scampered all over the back area as if discovering it for the first time. Leah came up behind him and wrapped her arms around his slender waist. She leaned her head against his broad back, loving the feel of him. "Are you upset we didn't have a wedding?"

"I don't like weddings. So nope, not in the least." He pulled her around and tipped her face up to him. At six foot five, she always had to tip her head up to look him in the eye. "How about you, Leah? Are you mad I insisted on getting married at the court?"

"I would've married you in an airplane bathroom," she replied, sliding her hands up and down his back. "I just wanted you to be all mine."

The corners of his mouth twitched. It wasn't in Luke's nature to smile and a rarity that he laughed. She loved it, however, when there was a playful twinkle in his eyes and she looked forward to those moments between them.

He looked out through the open doorway. "I want my brother to be happy. He isn't."

"He'll have to figure it out himself, Luke. You can't take care of this for Tobias."

He nodded, brows knitted. "Yeah, I know."

"Want a glass of wine?" She pulled away and went to the kitchen counter where they kept wine glasses. "Or a beer?"

"Nope." He whistled and the little dogs hurried back inside. "I want you to do something."

Leah narrowed her eyes. "Like what?"

"Remember that time when you took advantage of me?"

Immediately, the picture was clear as day. Leah had been bold and had unzipped his pants, taken him into her mouth and not relented until he'd come.

Her breathing hitched. "Yeah, I might remember something."

"I think about it all the time." He signaled for the dogs to go to their little crates and they scampered away.

"Come here, Leah."

She wanted to banter a bit more but, already, heat pooled and she wasn't going to be able to hold out long. She licked her lips. "You taste better than wine."

A visible bulge formed behind his zipped jeans and he slid a hand down the front. "Do you know what I want?"

"Yeah, now it's getting clearer," Leah said, following his movements. She went to him and unbuttoned his jeans. "I'm going to need you to cooperate fully, Mr. Hamilton."

CHAPTER TWENTY-ONE

THE THUMPING OF Tori's heart echoed in her ears. At this rate, she'd pass out before ever getting to Tobias' place. It had been three entire days since she'd seen him last and she had barely slept a wink. Her mind had gone over every detail of what he'd said.

Love. He loved her. It had taken a lot of courage for him to come clean and declare how he felt without asking for anything in return. If anything, judging by the way they'd been getting along over the years, it was more likely she'd shove him over the edge of the hill than to agree to consider what he'd said.

Of course she loved him. That went without saying. She'd tried so hard to keep that part of her hidden, but the way he'd looked at her, with so much sincerity, had melted all her resolve away.

She'd gone home and paced for half the night. Then tossed and turned in bed unable to decide what to do. First thing the next day, she'd called Alec and ended things. He'd been disappointed, but wished her well. It wouldn't be fair to continue a relationship when her heart wouldn't be in it.

Now, still not sure, she drove to see Tobias. A part of her wanted to believe in happily ever after, and that they'd fall into a perfect, loving relationship. The other half of her feared the ramifications of the secret she'd kept from him and the resentment over his abandonment when he'd left to go overseas.

She'd done some stupid shit back then and, like most mistakes, they'd come back to bite her in the ass.

His house came into view. The cabin-style home was huge. The architecture reminded her of the beautiful homes that graced the covers of log cabin magazines. She'd gone there often when dating Tobias and knew the layout by heart. The immense front room, the expansive kitchen and the upstairs bedroom where she and Tobias had pretended to study.

She imagined he slept downstairs now that he lived there alone. Up until Taylor had moved in with Allison, the two had been roommates for years.

Luke had also lived there for a few months, but he and Leah had fallen in love quickly and he'd moved in with her.

So now it was just Tobias and his two labs from what she understood.

She pulled up and cut off the engine, the entire time listening for the barks of alert or for someone to notice, but it was quiet. A quick glance at her watch told it was only six in the evening. The ranch hands must have gone home.

Tori let out a breath, grabbed her purse and climbed out of the car. When she reached the front door, it was slightly open, as if he expected someone.

She rang the doorbell, expecting dogs to come barking, but there was no reply. Immediately, her mind went haywire. What if something had happened? Or maybe he'd left in a hurry. No, that wasn't it. His truck was parked on the side of the house.

"Come in," Tobias called out from somewhere in the house.

Gingerly, she pushed the door open and stepped into the dim interior. The entry and front rooms were just like she remembered. There were newer leather couches that flanked a large stone fireplace, side tables, which were made out of dark thick wood, held lamps and nothing else.

Above the fireplace was a huge flat screen TV. An old western movie was playing on it. She continued past to the kitchen, which again hadn't changed much except the appliances were now stainless steel instead of black. Every surface was pristine. The house smelled of recently being cleaned. *Interesting.*

Deep laughter got her attention and she followed the sound to the back patio through open doors. The doors were different. They used to be sliders, but now they were French doors that were swung open.

Just past the furnished patio was Tobias. He threw two balls and his dogs took after them. Two plump little puppies attempted to follow suit. When they tripped over their own feet and began tumbling over each other, Tobias laughed. He guffawed so hard he was bent at the waist.

"Go get...the...balls," he sputtered, only to lose it when the puppies tried to attack one of the larger dogs.

Finally, he regained his composure long enough to take the balls from the older dogs and throw them again. Once again, the excited puppies yapped. But this time, they ran in circles and Tobias began laughing again.

Tori couldn't help but smile. She'd not seen him so relaxed in years. How could she have forgotten this side of him? Tobias was the most easy-going of the trio. Between Luke's intensity and Taylor's quiet nature, it was always Tobias who broke the ice and went out of his way to make friends.

"Hey, man, grab a beer," he called out over his shoulder. Obviously, he was expecting a guy to stop by. "Watch this," he said and threw a ball.

The puppies yapped happily and rushed after it only to lose interest and chase after a branch. Tobias chuckled. "They can't fetch for crap."

"That's because they're babies," Tori replied and smiled when he jerked around to her.

"I thought you were Eric."

"Sorry." She put her purse down on a chair and crouched down to greet the puppies. "You got the puppies. Why did you do that?" she looked into his eyes.

He shrugged. "I've got space. Besides, they'll earn

their keep around here. Lots of work for a dog at the Hamilton ranch."

"I hear all Scamp and Duke do is sleep, eat and play," Tori teased. "Is that their job?"

He smiled in return. "Pretty much." The smile was replaced by a frown as he looked to the back door. "Want a beer? I don't have any wine."

"A beer sounds good. You expecting company then?"

He turned to her, his gaze moving over her. "Eric is coming to borrow a four wheeler. He may have already come and gone and didn't stop by here."

Tori shrugged. "I didn't see him on the way here."

He went inside and Tori lowered to a chair. She picked up a puppy and kissed its face and then did the same to the other one. They were both females, tan with white spots. She wondered if Tobias had already named them.

Male voices sounded from inside. It seemed Eric had arrived. Tobias brought her the beer. "Stay here, I'll be right back."

"Ok." She slumped. The last thing she needed was more time to think. Her nerves were already strung tighter than a guitar string.

Thankfully, the dogs distracted her for the next few minutes and she found herself laughing almost as hard as Tobias had been.

"Remembering the sound of your laughter was the one thing that always made me smile when I was away from here." She'd been so engrossed in playing with the dogs that she hadn't heard him return.

She turned to find him, beer in hand, leaning against the doorjamb studying her. "Every time you mention being overseas, I feel like crap for what I did."

"You shouldn't. I was heartbroken, but not to the point that I'd do something stupid. Besides, after a couple months, I got an assignment away from the battlefield. I got lucky, I gue…" He didn't finish the sentence, his gaze going toward where Luke lived. Unlike him, his brother had been in the midst of battle, not just assigned once, but several times.

"You did your part," Tori said, lifting a puppy and pointing it to him. "You're definitely this little one's hero."

He looked at her for a long time before his gaze moved to the little dog and his lips curved. "She's a cutie."

"She is. Have you named them yet?"

Tobias walked out to the patio. "Not yet. Help me with that."

"Sure." Tori wasn't sure how to start the conversation. "I always wanted to name a daughter Piper. How about if we name her Piper?"

Something about his countenance changed when he lowered to sit. He leaned forward. "What if you have a daughter? You won't want to name her after my dog."

"True," she replied noncommittally. Although she'd not planned to have children, the possibility did come to mind every once in a while. However, at the moment, she didn't want to think about children. Overseas assignments and children were two subjects that were touchy between them.

"She looks like a rascal. So she needs a name that's fitting." Tori put the puppy down and immediately it took off running after the other one. The bundles of fur kept their attention for a bit.

"I was thinking Catsup and Mustard," Tobias said, his gaze still on the little dogs.

"That's stupid."

"Salt and Pepper?"

"No."

Tori clapped. "What about Tango and Waltz."

"Now that is super stupid."

"Ugh. I can't think."

Tobias chuckled. "I'm not responding to that one."

"Bella and Stella," Tori said with a grin. "I think that suits them."

He studied her for a long moment. "They could be your pups and you can name them whatever you want."

The air sizzled between them as Tori struggled with an appropriate response. He wasn't smiling and his gaze darkened as it traveled to her lips.

"I meant what I said the other day, Tori. I want us to try. You are it for me. If you don't want me, then I'm done."

The declaration took her breath away. How was it possible that after all these years, he would finally admit to his feelings so freely?

"What if things don't work out, Tobias? What if after all this time, it's too late?"

He stood and neared, and then pulling her to her feet and tipped her face up. "That's just it. I don't want to lose any more time. We're both stubborn as hell and I know how scary this is for you. I mean, it wasn't easy to admit how I feel."

"I admire you for it," she whispered. And then she allowed herself the freedom to wrap her arms around his waist. "Oh, Tobias, I don't know that I'm as brave. I am so scared of the resentment you have to have for me. I was wrong on so many levels."

He placed his cheek on the top of her head. "I don't resent you. Not you, right now. The nineteen-year-old Tori, now her I don't like very much."

She couldn't help but chuckle. "She was an idiot."

The deep rumble in his chest when he laughed made her smile. It was time to take a chance to let the true feelings take over. Perhaps they would crash and burn. Who knew for sure? But Tori agreed with him. She didn't want to lose any more time or moments.

"I love you," she said into his chest. "I have always loved you, even when I hated you, I loved you."

"I know," Tobias quipped, jumping when she pinched his side. "Ow. That hurt."

Tori laughed. "You had no clue."

"I know that when I enter a room you always straighten. You keep an eye on me when I am around and you defended me once."

She looked up at him with brows drawn. "Defended you?"

"Yep." Tobias nodded. "Taylor told me that one day people were saying that I wasn't good enough to run this ranch on my own and you jumped in and stood up for me."

After a long breath, Tori shrugged. "It's one thing for me to be mean to you. Anyway, it's the truth. I know you have a steady head for business."

"You love me?" His expression was a combination of awe and happiness. The way his eyes shined made Tori want to hug him tighter.

"Yes, Tobias, I may as well admit it. There were many times I wished I didn't."

When his mouth covered hers, Tori wanted to devour him, to take everything he had to give and even more. It wasn't enough, not by a long shot. If only she could freeze the moment forever. The warmth of the sun on them, the steady cool breeze and the wonderful feeling of his hard body so tightly against her were overwhelming.

More. She needed to be skin-to-skin, to feel the length of his limbs entangled with hers.

"Make love to me, Tobias." She got the words out between kisses. Each time he pulled up just a bit, she pulled him down for more. The hunger was uncontrollable, every fiber of her being screaming for his touch and kiss.

He closed the doors as they worked their way into

the house. "The dogs will be fine, there's water and places for them to chill."

There could have been a raging storm and Tori would barely notice. In two steps, Tobias swooped her up in his arms and stalked to the bedroom, one she'd never been in before.

It was classically Tobias. A huge bed centered on the widest wall and a dresser across from it with a giant flat screen tv above it. In the corner were two large dog beds and other than a side table on one side of the bed, that was the extent of the furnishings.

Once again, he took her mouth with his and while trailing kisses down from her neck to her shoulders, Tobias unbuttoned her blouse. Tori tugged at his shirt and once he dragged it up over his head, she almost cried at the beauty of him.

Her fingers itched to trace over every muscle and ripple. Losing control, she tugged off her shorts while he removed his jeans and, without hesitation, they crashed against one another, excited at the prospect of what was to come.

The prodding of his erection against her stomach only added to Tori's excitement, her breaths short and quick. Tobias took his time, slid her to lie across the bed fully naked and on display for him to take in.

His lips curved. "I am going to apologize now for what is going to be a quick release."

Tori stretched her arms to him. "I want you too much to wait."

And then he came over her, the large heaviness of him so very perfect while at the same time sending her senses so high, she dug her fingers into his shoulders and down his back. It was as if by some strange instance, they could absorb into one another and become one.

Tobias understood her need, but he teased her, his mouth moving away from hers to suck in her left nipple. At the same time, he toyed with the other pert peak.

A moan escaped and Tori bit her bottom lip to keep from screaming. Not that anyone could hear them, but she didn't want to alarm the dogs.

Moving to take in the other breast, Tobias licked and suckled it. This time, his free hand moved down her stomach to between her legs, which she eagerly parted for him.

The man knew exactly what to do and, within moments, she was spiraling out of control, no longer able to keep from crying out as she tumbled down from heights, she didn't remember existed.

When he drove into her, Tori was already out of control. Her entire body trembled at the wonderful sensation. He thrust in and pulled out only to drive back in, hard and fast, just like she loved it.

"Yes!" Tori screamed, unable to keep from thrashing as a wonderful rush of heat surged from where they were connected down her legs and back up to her stomach.

"Oh my God." Tori tried her best to not climax again, wanting to wait for him, but her eyelids fluttered closed as stars sparkled behind her eyes.

In the fog of delight, she heard his deep moan as he found release and, moments later, his weight crushed atop her.

Tori couldn't form a coherent thought. Her entire being was still shaking from the strength of her last orgasm.

"Tobias," she whispered, kissing his damp temple. "That had to be the most amazing sex I've ever had."

He'd not pulled out and she dug her fingers into his butt to keep him in place.

"Mmmm." Tobias lifted up just enough to look at her. "I have to agree with that."

There was a slight twitch. He was getting hard again. Tori let out a contented sigh. "Good. I was about to ask if we could do it again."

THE PUPPIES WOKE Tobias. They were whining and scratching at the crate, wanting to be let out.

"You two are going to be trouble," he whispered at them. Both sat side by side and cocked their heads to the side.

Although groggy, he smiled. "Okay, that's cute."

Tori let out a sigh and continued to sleep and he peered at her. She wore a short pixie cut, but it was disheveled and adorable. When they'd dated before, her hair had been almost to her waist. He decided he liked it short.

Her lips were pursed in slumber, begging for a man's kiss. He would have obliged if not for a second set of puppy whines.

"Okay. I'm coming." He slid from the bed and pulled on a pair of sweats. Instead of opening the door and letting the pups out, he reached in and picked them up. After a couple times of them peeing as soon as he let them out, he'd figured out it was a bad idea.

When he came back inside with the puppies on his heels, Tobias poured kibbles into bowls. The two larger dogs looked up from their dog beds, which had been moved to the kitchen, not at all interested in the goings-on.

He slipped back into the bed and snuggled against Tori. Her slight body was warm and supple. Instantly, he wanted to plunge into her again. She was the only woman who could make him lose control to the point of almost passing out. The night before had been an awakening of sorts, not just sexual, but emotional. It made Tobias understand the difference between regular sex and being intimate with someone he cared deeply for.

Things were totally different when the heart was involved.

"Good morning," Tori mumbled, turning to him and nuzzling his neck. "I don't want to deal with reality."

He slid his hands down her back, cupping her round bottom. "Me, either."

"And yet we both do," she stretched, her delicious curves melting against him. "What time is it?"

"Seven. It's Saturday. You don't have to get up early, do you?"

"Yep, have to be at the restaurant at nine to be ready for the lunch crowd."

When she started to move away, he pulled her close again. "We're good, right?" Tobias grimaced at hearing the fear in his voice. Damn, he was turning into an emotional sap or something.

She cupped his jaw and smiled. "Totally."

"So I can call you twenty times a day and you'll come here tonight?"

After a soft kiss that sent tingles down his spine, she slipped out of his arms. "Dinner isn't over until ten. By the time we clean up, it's midnight. I will be bushed."

"So?"

She chuckled. "So you have two puppies to care for. I have a restaurant. You have cows. I have hungry diners. We'll have to work it out."

"I didn't think about all that." He sat up and scratched the stubble on his jaw. "We're going to have to figure out the logistics. Tomorrow then?"

Tori had already pulled on her clothes. She climbed back onto the bed and leaned against his chest. "The restaurant is closed tomorrow. We can spend the whole day together."

"Good." He huffed when there was scratching at the door. "Those two are going to drive me bonkers."

Tori laughed and went to the door. The puppies raced in and ran in circles, yapping. She picked them up and put them on the bed. "There's your daddy."

Delighted, they scampered to him and began licking his face. Tobias pushed them away gently and they ran back, enjoying the game.

"I'll see you tomorrow. Call you later." Tori was heading out the door, but he wasn't about to let her go that easily.

Tobias caught her at the front door and spun her around. "Maybe you should call in sick."

"My boss is a bitch," Tori quipped. "Kiss me good-bye."

He took her mouth and kissed her until she moaned. "Tobias…no…mmm…oh no you don't." Tori firmly pushed away and he allowed it.

"Call me." She slid out the door and dashed down the front steps to her car.

A few moments later, Tobias caught himself standing in the same spot with a wide grin. He was an idiot. But damn, he was a happy one.

CHAPTER TWENTY-TWO

ALLISON'S MOUTH OPENED and closed. Her wide eyes locked with Tori's. "Oh." She managed after a few beats. "You and Tobias finally…" she looked to Leah whose expression was almost identical.

"That's why I wanted to tell you both at the same time, because I knew you'd be speechless," Tori said and the sipped from her wine glass.

They were at Luke and Leah's house. They'd decided to meet there to discuss and plan a new event for the new community project they were heading.

"When's the wedding?" Leah asked, her gaze soft. "It's so romantic. I can't wait to see you both together."

Tori sighed. "It is romantic. You won't believe the change in him."

"Speak of Dr. Jekyll, he just pulled up," Allison said, motioning to the huge front window of the living room.

Sure enough, Tobias was climbing out of his truck and placed the puppies down. Luke walked over from whatever he was doing.

"Don't make a big deal," Tori warned. "We've only been a couple for two weeks. So we're still getting used to things."

"I'm so excited," Leah said with a wide smile. "You guys were meant to be."

Allison high-fived Leah. "I told you the other day, didn't I?"

"Told her what?" Tori narrowed her eyes.

"That something was afoot," Allison replied with a grin. "You are glowing and shit."

When the twins walked in, Tori couldn't tear her eyes from them. They were so alike and yet so different. Luke was bulkier, his expression always cautious, as if always on alert. Tobias, on the other hand, had a more relaxed demeanor.

Luke looked to them and scowled. Leah and Allison held their wine glasses halfway to their lips, eyes moving between Tori and Tobias.

"What's going on?" Luke asked no one in particular and Tobias nudged him with his elbow.

"Let's grab a beer and go out back. The puppies are digging."

Everyone turned and, sure enough, Bella and Stella were making good progress on a hole. Leah gasped. "So much for my garden. You better go out there and stop those two."

Tobias winked at Tori and walked through the living area and past the kitchen to the back. Meanwhile, Luke made a beeline for the refrigerator.

"They're so cute," Allison said, grinning.

"The puppies?" Leah asked.

"Yes, but that's not who I was referring to. After all these years, I am still shaken up when I see them together. So identical," Allison remarked.

Leah laughed. "I can tell the difference immediately. Luke is cuter."

Both looked at Tori who shrugged. "I can tell who's who, and I think Tobias has a bit of an edge in the good looks department."

Luke cleared his throat. "Seriously? That's what you three still talk about? Boys."

"Yep," all three replied in unison.

He walked out to where Tobias was attempting to keep the puppies from returning to their project.

"I DIDN'T KNOW you'd be over at my brother's," Tobias said that night. It was early evening, the sun not yet setting. Tobias was setting up a pen of sorts in a closed in area he'd built on the back deck. It would be where Bella and Stella would stay whenever he left the ranch. They were not quite yet potty trained and he didn't like crating them for long periods.

Tori neared and peered down. "Wow, I'm almost jealous of them. Plush beds, toys and rawhides. Plus enough room for them to play and be out of the elements if it rains."

He crawled out of the enclosure. "Knowing those two, they'll drag everything out into the rain and scratch at the back door."

"True," Tori said and laughed.

When he whistled, all four dogs raced from wherever they were and looked to Tobias, obviously expecting treats. He picked up the puppies and placed them in the enclosure. They ran in circles, tumbling over each other to fight over a toy.

"Let's see how long that lasts." Tobias sat in a chair and watched them. There was a clear Plexiglas top over the enclosure, which had three solid wooden walls and the front of it was a metal fence. He didn't close the door so the puppies could go in and out.

"Looks like they like it so far." He held out a hand to Tori. "Come here. You seem pensive."

She sat on his lap and snuggled against his chest. "I have been thinking."

It was interesting when he stiffened. Tori hated how he always seemed to expect bad news from her. "About?"

"I am considering selling the restaurant."

"What would you do with your time?"

"I want to explore other things. I've been tied to that place for so long, I've not traveled or gone to visit family as often as I would like. I haven't seen my brother in months."

"What about income?" Tobias asked and then let out a long breath. "Does this mean you want to leave Laurel Creek?"

She giggled and kissed his jaw. "Never. I am not allowing you out of my sight. It took us too long to get our shit together. I have a good amount in savings plus I'll have the restaurant money."

Tobias relaxed. "Why don't you move in with me? You're always here anyway."

"Are you serious?" Tori straightened to meet his gaze. "How long before we have a fight and you kick me out?" She laughed. "We haven't been friends long enough I don't think."

He kissed and nuzzled neck. "I think we get along just fine."

Tingles of desire ran down from where his lips touched her skin. "Don't do that while I'm trying to think. I get distracted," Tori protested weakly.

Tobias lifted his head and met her gaze. "All right, talk. Tell me what you're thinking. How can I help?"

She bit her bottom lip. "Right now, my plan is to offer Marco ownership. I want to take a couple years to relax, travel and, hopefully, convince you to go to Paris with me."

"Sounds good so far." Tobias nodded. "What do you think you want to do after that?"

"Owning a business takes too many hours. It's a commitment that I'm a bit tired of. I have a degree in marketing, so maybe I'll do something with that. I'll take a few courses to familiarize myself with what's new."

Tobias grinned. "Sounds good. But right now, I have something I really need to take care of. Can we finish talking later?" He pushed her to stand and got up. "Come with me."

The smell of whatever was cooking in the slow cooker welcomed them when they entered the kitchen. Tobias closed the French doors and turned to her. "I'm horny as all get out."

Tori laughed. "So what else is new?" She took his hand and led him to the bedroom. Tobias' heated gaze followed her every move as she slipped from the sundress she wore. In her bra and panties, she motioned to him. "Undress."

Lying atop the bedding, she enjoyed the show of how his muscles bunched and leveled with each move as he pulled his t-shirt off over his head and then pushed his jeans and briefs down. On full display, he was mouth-watering.

But there would be no foreplay. Instinctively, she knew that and it was exactly how she wanted him. Hard and fast, no games. Already, her core burned with yearning and she removed her panties. "Hurry," she more panted than said.

He came to her and yanked her legs to the edge of the bed, then held his penis and nudged between them. There was an intensity about him that could be described as almost lethal when he was intent on taking her. Tori squirmed at being open for him to gaze upon.

Thankfully, he didn't make her wait, knowing she'd climax almost instantly. He positioned himself at her entry and grunted. The purr as enticing as the man.

And then he plunged.

Tori screamed, her body quaking as he drove into her over and over until she lost control.

"Roll over." Tobias guided Tori to all fours. They'd already climaxed once and, this time, he would take his time and use her body to find his pleasure. She was more than willing. He entered her from behind, his hand moving between her folds and she gasped at how sensitive she'd become.

Tori couldn't do more than gasp and call out his name as he thrust in, filling her fully. "Damn, this feel so good," he grunted, taking her by the hips so he could push in again and again.

SHE WAS SPRAWLED across his chest, too weak to move. They were both slick with sweat and she loved the feeling of it.

Tobias' hands roved over her body absently. He kissed her hair and sighed. It was the contented sigh of a well-satisfied man.

"I want you to move in, Tori. I want you here with me."

Tori nodded. "I know and maybe after the restaurant sells, I will. Right now it would be too hard. I need to be there all the time and it's nice to have my place so close when I get little breaks."

"Yeah, I get that."

"So I'm not saying no," Tori said. "Let me just take

care of this restaurant business. Okay?"

She pressed a kiss to the center of his chest. "I want to live with you. I want to be part of Bella and Stella's lives."

"What about Duke and Scamp? Don't you love them?" Tobias pretended to be hurt.

"Them, too," Tori said.

EPILOGUE

Six months later

ALLISON HAD BEEN grinning so hard all day that her face threatened to crack. She couldn't tear her eyes away from Taylor. In a tuxedo, surrounded his cousins, he was laughing at something someone said. The men then stopped talking as the photographer urged them to pose for another of a string of pictures.

The wedding had grown from a family gathering to a full out wedding with two hundred guests.

The Laurel Creek reception hall was filled with many people. Since she owned the flower shop in town, and Taylor was Laurel Creek's sheriff, it seemed natural to invite many of the locals to attend their wedding.

Thankfully, between the Hamilton family and her parents, the costs had been divided and there was plenty of food, music and drink for so many guests.

She'd moved to a table with Mindy, Leah and Tori waited for their turn to take pictures. Eric and Ernest's parents were at an adjoining table, happily conversing with Luke and Tobias' parents. She was struck by how handsome the older Hamilton men remained. They had good genes.

"Here comes the photographer," Leah said with a grin. "The last of the pictures hopefully."

"I want to get some shots of each couple," the woman said, looking at Tori. "You first since it's your husband's idea."

Allison giggled. "Go to your *husband*," she said, emphasizing the word.

"WE'RE NOT MARRIED," Tori explained unnecessarily since the woman was already walking away.

"You will be soon," someone called out as she walked away. Tori chuckled.

After pictures, which she was glad for since Tobias looked so attractive in his black tux, she thought of how good they looked together. She wore a soft pink floral dress that flowed down to her ankles. The picture would definitely be framed and put up at the family home they now shared.

Tobias hugged her close and led her to the dance floor where they began swaying to a slow, jazzy number. She sighed and looked up at him with butterflies in her stomach. "This is a beautiful wedding. I can't imagine those two with anyone but each other. They are so in love."

"The Hamiltons are all done for," Tobias quipped,

looking to where his twin and Leah were now being posed for pictures. He chuckled. "Luke looks like he's in pain."

Tori had to agree. "He's come far though. I would never have imagined the man that returned to Montana, so angry and broken, doing that. Posing for a couple's picture."

"You're right," Tobias said and kissed her gently. "Luke has certainly changed since his return."

The rest of the evening was magical and although Tori had to talk to Tobias, give him news that could potentially ruin the evening, she kept putting it off.

Tomorrow. She would wait one more day. After all, what difference would it make?

"Toast." Someone handed her a glass of champagne when they returned to the table. Five couples stood in a circle. Leah and Luke, Allison and Taylor, Mindy and Eric, Henry and Ernest and then her and Tobias all held their glasses up.

"What are we toasting?" Tori asked, lifting her glass and unsuccessfully doing her best to keep her hand from trembling.

"Love, silly," Allison said with a wide smile, "and also happiness."

"Here, here!" everyone said at once and sipped.

Tori's stomach revolted as soon as the sip of champagne hit it. She couldn't put it off any longer. Tugging at Tobias' hand, she got his attention.

"We need to talk," she whispered when he lowered.

"It's important."

Immediately, the guarded expression shuttered his features. "Right now?"

Tori swallowed. No going back now. Besides, hopefully, he wouldn't yell at her with this many people around.

They walked out of the billowing tent to a cusp of trees. She let out a shaky sigh and, for some reason, immediately began to cry.

Tobias wrapped his arms around her. "What's wrong? Are you sick?"

"Not really sick per se," she sniffed. "I don't know how you're going to take this. I wanted to wait but I can't keep it to myself any longer. I've been feeling sick to my stomach. I was scared that I had an ulcer or something. So I went to the doctor." Tears began flowing in earnest and she wiped at them impatiently.

"I am four months pregnant," she blurted out the words as relief washed over her. Even if Tobias didn't want children, she was excited at a second chance. "It's twins," she finished weakly.

Tobias let out such a loud yell, people rushed from the tent to see what had happened. Luke was the first to approach at an all-out sprint. "What the fuck?" he said at noting Tobias' wide grin.

"Babies." Tobias said then looked at Tori's barely showing stomach. "She's got babies."

Luke scowled and turned to find not only Leah, but also Allison, Taylor and Eric had come. At noticing

Tobias' smile, other guests who'd looked out, returned to the party.

Tobias' mother neared and hugged Tori. "What does he mean by babies?"

"I'm...I'm expecting twins," Tori replied, crying again. "I just found out yesterday."

"Twins." Tobias scowled. "And you waited this long to tell me?"

"I wanted to wait until after the wedding. I was so nervous, I didn't think I could get pregnant." She sniffed. "I thought maybe you'd be mad and break things off."

Luke shoved Tobias. "You would break up with her if she got pregnant?"

"No," Tobias shoved him back. "I'm going to marry her."

"Good," Luke said. "She'll say yes."

The women watched the interaction between the twins, especially when they went silent and seemed to communicate with just looks.

Congratulations, I'm happy for you.

Thanks, love you, Brother.

Back at ya.

Everyone understood Tobias and Tori needed a moment and returned to the wedding.

"I can't believe it," Tobias said and lifted Tori up circling. "Thank you. I love you."

"Put me down before I puke," Tori protested weakly.

He did and held her hand pulling her further away from the wedding tent. "This time it will be different. Our twins will grow up at the ranch and we'll make sure they are safe."

Tori sniffed and nodded. "I am certain of it."

They looked into each other's eyes for a long moment until Tobias scowled. "My mother will want to move in and take over."

Just then Mrs. Hamilton appeared. "Tori, did I see you drink champagne?"

Both broke out laughing.

Dear Reader,

Writing is my dream come true, I enjoy sharing my stories with you. Hopefully you enjoyed Tobias and Tori's story. I enjoyed writing the banter between these two.

I am not sure if this series will continue. I do have an idea for Alex Hamilton who is on his way to Laurel Creek, but we'll see.

I love hearing from you and am always excited when readers join my newsletter list. It's the best way to keep abreast of new releases and other things happening in my world. You can also follow me on Facebook and Instagram.

Newsletter:
landing.mailerlite.com/webforms/landing/t7e4q0

Facebook:
facebook.com/AuthorHildieMcQueen

Instagram:
instagram.com/hildiemcqueenwriter

Email:
mailto:Hildie@HildieMcQueen.com

Website:
www.HildieMcQueen.com